I LOVE YOU
BILLY LANGLEY

Monika Jephcott-Thomas

Clink
Street

London | New York

Published by Clink Street Publishing 2019

Copyright © 2019
First edition.

ISBN:s
978-1-912850-68-6 paperback
978-1-912850-69-3 ebook

To my wonderful children and grand children

May your lives be full of adventures, new beginnings with each part being better than the last.

May you give each other strength.

May your choices be good ones and if they prove not to may you have the courage to change them.

I hope you will be happy and safe, surrounded by people who love you and treat you well.

Please always know and remember how much I love you.

Mum/Omama

ACKNOWLEDGEMENTS

Thanks again to the team for all they have done to get the book published.

Many thanks again to Warren Fitzgerald whose support is invaluable.

Marc Allington to you many thanks as well because without your ingenuity there would be no cover design.

Finally to my husband Jeff for his steady love and encouragement.

1

Netta Portner looked around her bedroom as if it were the last time she would ever see it. It wasn't. Not just yet. But she felt the need to capture everything in her memory now, before the chaos of leaving ensued and clouded everything. As she scanned the room she caught sight of herself in the mirror on the dressing table. She turned to face her reflection, smoothed down her dress, adjusted her glasses, and raised her chin in the confident manner she prayed she could adopt when she stood in front of a class of comprehensive school students next week in the south of England.

'Here!' Her mother came hurrying into the room, dumping three suitcases of various sizes onto the bed.

To Netta the hurrying and dumping seemed completely unnecessary and typically dramatic. For a split second Netta wondered if it was designed to mask a sadness at her imminent departure from the nest, but that notion was soon buried under her general irritation with her mother, which Netta had cultivated throughout her teenage years.

'These served me well when I moved here from Kunzendorf,' said her mother.

'During the war? When you were pregnant with me?' Netta asked, delighting in her albeit embryonic presence in the story her mother had regaled her with on many occasions – the story of an arduous journey all the way across a devastated Germany on its knees in the final months of the Second World War. Since then Netta had never been much farther from home than the north coast for family holidays.

'Hm-mm!' her mother sang her response as noncha-lantly as she could. 'So a little jaunt to England should present no issue for them.'

'It's hardly a little jaunt, Mama.'

'Well it's hardly a race across a vast nation being bombed mercilessly by the Allies either, is it?' her mother said.

Netta seethed as she flipped open the lid of each case.

Her mother, hands on hips, looked around the room as if she had never seen it before. 'At last I can give this room a damn good clean.'

Netta looked daggers at her mother's back as she ran her finger along the chest of drawers and grimaced at the dust she found there.

'Oh please, mother! When was the last time you cleaned anything?'

'Well, I'll get Emilia to do it. Chuck out all this rubbish too.'

'Hey! There's no rubbish in here. And don't you go telling Emilia to throw anything away. This is my stuff. My room.'

'You're moving to England. So how can this be your room anymore?'

'I might be back… for the holidays.'

'Oh, Anetta, either you're going or you're staying, do make up your mind!'

'So you don't want me to come for Christmas?'

'What I want has nothing to do with it, clearly. You'll do whatever you want, as usual.'

'Whatever I want! That's a laugh.' Netta muttered the next words only half-wanting them to be heard. 'I can't wait to be free.'

'What was that? Free, you say? You want to be free? And what's that supposed to mean exactly?'

There was a lifetime of gripes Netta could have listed to answer her mother, but instead she pouted, 'Nothing.' Then like the child her mother could always draw out of her just as her mother drew pus from her patients' cysts, Netta whined, 'Mama?'

'Yes?' her mother said in a tone which suggested she'd

2

forgotten there was another woman in the room and only heard her baby in need.

Netta stared into the open cases as if they were bottomless. 'What does one pack for a whole new country?'

Her mother tutted. 'Well, that my dear, is for you to work out. I'm far too busy with the surgery to worry about things like that.'

Netta looked up from the cases when she heard her mother's voice tremble, but she couldn't see her face as she was already stomping out of the room.

Two of the suitcases were now full; the smallest would be packed with the things she still needed in the last couple of days before she left for England, such as the makeup she now applied to her cheeks and the perfume she dabbed on her wrists and neck as she got ready to go out with her friends on what she was both excited and sad to hear them call a farewell drink.

She bounded down the two flights of stairs in the large house her parents had built in Mengede – big enough to accommodate the doctor's surgery they ran together as well as both sets of Netta's grandparents without them getting under each other's feet; something which her mother's parents had always been particularly keen on since they reluctantly came to live here nearly a decade ago. However, at mealtimes in the dining room this was not always possible. Hence Netta was more than happy to have an excuse not to join the family for dinner this evening, but she could not avoid the dining room altogether because her grandfather Karl was in there and he had something she needed.

'Good evening everyone,' she said as she came in, relaxing a little when she realised her other grandfather Gerhard was not present. 'Hello, Opa,' she said kissing Karl on the top of his white hair.

'Want to borrow the car by any chance?' Karl smiled up

at her, then winked at Frieda, Gerhard's wife, who didn't seem to find it in the least bit amusing as she carried on slurping up her soup.

'Oh, yes please,' Netta said with pantomime surprise at the idea.

Karl fished the keys from his pocket and dangled them over his plate.

'Now we know the real reason for that kiss,' Martha said with a warm laugh.

'No, Oma!' Netta said to her other grandmother, theatrically putting her hands on her hips. 'You know that's not true.'

'Go! And have a great time!' Karl said handing her the keys.

'Thanks, Opa,' Netta beamed and turned to leave when her Omi Frieda piped up, 'Where are you going?'

Netta froze. Cursed inwardly. Hung a smile over her annoyance and turned back, leaning in the doorway as casually as she could. 'Just out with my friends.'

'Looking like that?'

'Like what?' Netta glanced down at herself, at her light summer dress and pointed shoes with mid-heels.

'Like a prostitute,' her Omi said, pulling her own cardigan around her with her free hand as if to make sure she was not in danger of looking the same.

'Oh, Frieda,' Martha protested.

'Yes,' Netta said unfazed. 'Oh, Omi! When exactly was the last time you saw a prostitute?'

'About five seconds ago it seems. You're supposed to be a teacher. What would your students say if they saw you looking like that?'

Netta tutted loudly. 'So teaching is a respectable profession now, is it, Omi?' Frieda frowned at Netta, a little baffled, so Netta elucidated. 'The way you used to go on about Opa and Oma being *just* teachers you would have thought *they* were whores.'

'Now, Netta,' Karl warned his granddaughter, though he flashed a wounded look at Frieda.

Frieda opened her withered lips in an to attempt to excuse what everyone knew was true, but was stopped by her husband's voice as he strode into the room grabbing Netta by the arms and moving her out of his way.

'Don't speak to your Omi like that!' he growled at Netta, then sat down and unpacked his satchel of its considerable number of important looking files.

'But she—' Netta had no idea what she was going to say in her defence since she knew her Opi and Omi shared the same views on just about everything, so she was relieved to be interrupted.

'Who is *she*? *She* is the cat's mother,' Gerhard said looking only at his files. 'Your Omi deserves a little more respect, young lady.'

'Do you need to do that here?' Martha pleaded with Gerhard as he spread his papers about the large teak table which could seat twelve.

'There's plenty of room. It's just the four of us,' he said. 'Or would you rather keep us locked out of sight in our pokey room upstairs?'

'How many times have we heard this!' Karl sighed. 'It's hardly pokey, Gerhard, come on.'

'But it's not quite the suite that you are treated to above the surgery, is it now,' Gerhard shrugged, 'even though this is my daughter's house.'

'Well, it's our son's house too, in case you hadn't noticed,' Martha said, 'And I think both Erika and Max have been very generous to us all over the years, making a home for us like this.'

'This is not my home,' Gerhard said sifting through his papers. 'This is hardly a dignified set up for a high ranking military officer and entrepreneur. My home is a stately villa nestled among majestically rolling hills, thank you very much.'

'Then why aren't you living in your stately villa and nestling among your majestically rolling hills now?' Netta said spitefully.

'Because,' Gerhard said stabbing with his finger at one of the documents, 'as you well know, the bloody Russians took everything we had, that's why. And someone's going to pay when I finally get my day in court.'

'Well, it seems to be us that are paying for it now, Opi,' Netta smiled.

'Such a rude girl!' Gerhard barked.

'She's just a teenager,' Martha said in her defence. 'Gerhard, please tidy up those papers.'

'Is this your house?'

'Well, you said it wasn't yours.'

'I'm not a teenager, Oma.'

'Teenager! There were no teenagers in my day,' Frieda said. 'You were a child or an adult. Teenager! That's just an excuse to be irresponsible.'

'I'm twenty. So how can I be a teenager? Maths not your strong point, Omi? You should have paid more attention to your *teachers*.'

'Still not too old to go over my knee, rude girl,' Gerhard shouted.

'Not surprising given her pedigree,' Frieda muttered, crumbs of bread flying from her wet lips.

'And what pedigree is that, Omi? My father is a doctor and his parents…' Netta said moving away from the door, coming back into the room and putting a protective arm on the shoulder of both Karl and Martha, '…were both highly respected teachers. You two were destitute after the war and the only people kind enough to offer you a roof over your heads and food in your bellies were these "commoners" and their son.'

'And my daughter,' Gerhard said petulantly.

'OK, that's enough,' Karl said gently. 'Let's all just eat, shall we?'

'Letting her go gallivanting in the car again, Karl?' Gerhard said.

'I said, enough, Gerhard please.'

'What's wrong with trains and buses, girl? If I have to use them, I can't see why you can't,' Gerhard said looking longingly at the car keys in Netta's hand.

'Where's Mama and Papa?' Netta said softly to one grandfather while glaring at the other.

'Your mother's out on home visits. Your father is finishing up in the surgery.'

'Papa should know about the way they speak to you.'

'And you should keep your opinions to yourself, young lady,' Gerhard said. 'It doesn't become… you.'

Netta read his hesitation and translated, 'You mean it doesn't become a woman?' She tutted again. 'Poor Omi! The only opinion you've ever been allowed is his, isn't it?'

Frieda looked like she might bring her soup back up and Gerhard stood, so Netta hurried out, knowing she had gone too far this time.

On her way out of the house, she decided, unusually, to go via the surgery. All the patients had gone for the day and her father, Max, was busy writing up notes.

'Hello, Papa!' She gave him a kiss on the head, just as she had given Karl. She wasn't usually so demonstrative with her father, but she felt especially protective of him right now after everything her Omi and Opi had said.

'Oh, what was that for?' he looked up with smiling eyes magnified through his round spectacles.

'I don't need a reason to kiss my papa, do I?'

Max shook his head and examined Netta with all the intensity of one who would not get to see his daughter for many months to come. 'What's up?'

'Nothing. Just Opi and Omi being crabby and ungrateful. Again.'

'Have you been arguing with them?'

'No. An argument would suggest there were two

opposing sides of a debate both with equal weight. There was nothing right about what they said. So I was just putting them straight,' she grinned.

'Netta,' Max smiled, 'give them a break. They've not had it easy.'

'Nor have you.'

'Gerhard was held in Siberia for eleven years.'

'And so were you.'

'For four years, yes.'

'Four years is a long time,' Netta said, burning to add that it felt like an eternity to her as a little girl without a father.

'Anyway, they're your mother's parents. We have to look after them as we do mine.'

Netta shrugged and played with the bulb on the blood pressure monitor which dangled from the desk.

'Going out?' Max asked.

'Yes. Out with the gang for a farewell drink.'

'Oh, good.' Max sat back in his chair. 'I'm so glad you have such good friends. You know, there was a little gang of five of us too, when we were at university. Your mother and I, Edgar, Kurt and… Horst.'

Netta knew his difficulty saying his oldest friend's name was due to the grief he still felt over losing Horst in the labour camp where they were both held after being captured by the Russians in the last days of the war, so she moved the conversation along quickly to try and spare him the pain.

'It's funny, you were all medical students. We're all teachers.'

'Yes.' Max took off his glasses and rubbed his eyes.

'But there are three girls in our gang. I can't believe Mama was the only woman in yours.'

'She was the only woman in the entire department, virtually. It wasn't the done thing for women to be doctors in those days.'

'Wow, that must have been... hard.'

'Oh yes, of course. In university and after when we came here to set up the surgery. Plenty of prejudice. But she's a strong and single-minded woman, your mother,' he said in a tone which seemed at once admiring and critical. 'A bit like her daughter,' he grinned.

2

She loved driving her grandfather's Lloyd. Despite its snazzy curves and two-tone paintwork it was known as the Cardboard Box because the bodywork was made of papier-mâché. Nevertheless, it was surprisingly strong and Netta, being the only one of her group of friends who had access to a car, felt a sense of pride to see the joy the others got from being whizzed about the place in it, though their arms and heads often poked out through the windows and sunroof of the little car. They all lived in Dortmund, the city to which Mengede was a suburb, and since the trains stopped running to and from Dortmund by 9 pm every night Netta would have been isolated without the use of the car. With it she enjoyed great sway over the gang's social plans and she had a preferred routine when it came to picking them all up, based not solely on geography. She picked up Anton first because he was always so cheerful, nothing it seemed could spoil his mood, so Netta always felt raring to party once Anton was in the car whatever her own mood was before. Next she would pick up Sophie. Sophie was the quietest of them all, but now Anton was in the car there would be no awkward silences for Netta to worry about. Next she would pick up Felix. She would have picked him up last if it hadn't been for Anna, but second to last would still ruffle him enough so they could all enjoy the look on his face – one of a boy left out of the game.

'Everything all right, Felix?' Anton said, sliding open the back seat window and grinning at his friend, who stood on the pavement smoking as casually as he could.

'Yes, why wouldn't it be?' Felix said opening the passenger door, lifting the front seat and squeezing himself in the back.

Netta looked over her shoulder and winked at Anton and Sophie, who stifled giggles like children at the back of their classes would, and then sped off to Anna's house.

Much as Netta would have loved to have left Felix until last, if she had, then they would all be waiting for Anna even longer than usual. If she was due at Felix's house at 7.15 pm, then that would mean she could be at Anna's by 7.30 pm. However, she would tell Anna on the phone earlier that day that she would be at her house at 7 pm and since Anna was always at least half an hour late for everything, they would hopefully only have to wait outside her house for five minutes before she swanned down the pathway as if she was Brigitte Bardot. Even for Netta's farewell drink, they all knew Anna would somehow make the evening all about her.

Ten minutes after Netta honked the horn, Anna got into the front passenger seat, smoothing down her long blonde hair, doing her best to look flustered and fabulous all at once. 'What a day!' she sighed.

'Why, what happened?' Sophie asked. The others winced. She was just being polite, but they knew it was better not to ask otherwise Anna would begin, as she did now, reeling off the catalogue of disasters that had beset her that day – from broken fingernails to her father's drinking and gambling problems. From her brothers annoying her to mountains of marking.

'You've had all summer to mark books,' Felix groaned.

'Oh please, Felix,' Anna said checking her lipstick in the wing mirror, 'I've got much better things to do with my summers than mark books.'

Anton exchanged a sarcastic look with Felix and said, 'So what have you been doing with your summer then, Anna? Or should I say, *who* have you been doing?'

Sophie let out a little squeak of shock before clamping her hand firmly over her mouth.

'Oh, my God,' Netta cried, 'I do not want to know. Spare me the details!'

But Anton persisted, 'Details, details, please! It's all in the detail.'

'None of your business,' Anna snapped.

The car was silent for a moment, but they all knew it wouldn't be long before Anna started plying them with details.

They went to a pub in Dortmund. Pubs were usually deemed to be too expensive for a night out. They would all, Anna excepted, much rather go to one of their houses for a little party and if it was anyone's house it would be Netta's since her parents had allowed her to use one of the cellars as a party room. The others thought Netta's parents were very cool to allow them to do this, though Netta knew it was partly because her parents would rather know where Netta was and that they believed she was safe if she was at home. Anton and Felix both worked part time in the Kronen Brewery and they had appropriated two empty beer barrels to use as tables in the cellar and some full ones to keep them supplied with cheap beer. So wherever they went, more often than not they would end up at Netta's house and this evening would be no exception. However, Felix insisted that for Netta's farewell drink they should at least splash out a little and have a round or two first in Wenker's Beer House. Anna seconded the motion, since she hadn't gone to all this effort to sit in a basement seen only by four friends. Netta was flushed with pride that they should agree to do this and grateful to Felix for the suggestion, which was, Anna said, exactly why Felix made the suggestion in the first place.

The pub still had the remnants of flags and bunting which the landlord, Herr Wenker, had enthusiastically decorated it with a month ago for the World Cup final between England and West Germany, most of which had been pulled down amid the disappointment of losing 4-2.

'And it was such a promising start too with the Helmut

Haller goal in only the twelfth minute,' Felix said to Anton, who seemed almost as uninterested as the girls, but Herr Wenker was more than happy to listen.

'I heard the Beatles stopped here for a drink on their way to Essen,' Anna said, drawing hard on her cigarette and scanning the room as she exhaled as if there was a chance George or Ringo may still be finishing up their lagers somewhere.

'Oh my God, you sound like one of my fifth-formers,' Netta said although she was more than partial to bit of the Fab Four herself.

As a conversation was sparked all around her about the relative merits of the rock 'n' roll band Netta felt a pang that the fifth-formers she mentioned would no longer be hers in any form next term.

'Is all that screaming really necessary?' Anton was saying.

'They ought to be locked up, these teenagers,' said Wenker.

'Feel free, that would do me a favour,' Anton smiled.

'Oh please,' said Anna, 'Everyone said there would be riots when the Beatles came and that didn't happen, did it?'

'It did in Hamburg,' countered Felix.

'That was not the fans, that was a group of rowdies, who were not remotely interested in the music, taking advantage of the situation.'

'Girls tearing off their clothes, fainting and getting hysterical? Sounds like a riot to me,' Wenker said.

'You members of the older generation particularly, who have lived through an era of fatal political hysteria, should be a bit more tolerant towards young people who are enthusiastic about rather harmless things,' said Sophie in Wenker's direction.

Everyone stopped and turned to look at her. It was the first thing she had said since they arrived. Netta grinned into her beer wondering how she would cope in England without this motley crew to educate and entertain her.

Back at Netta's house the gang settled in the cellar, the chat now feverish, fuelled by the beer and the rock 'n' roll on the record player.

'A toast,' said Anna, 'to our dear Netta. Not sure what I'm going to do without you to put me straight when I go wrong, but luckily that doesn't happen too often.'

Everyone snorted as required.

'Don't worry, Anna, I can help you with that in Netta's absence,' Anton smiled.

'But we wish you well,' Anna went on, 'and we're sure the British education system won't know what has hit it when you get stuck into it.'

'Hear, hear!' the others chimed in.

'Hurry back soon, won't you?' Anna looked as if she might cry so Netta gave her a big hug before the others gathered around to embrace Netta too.

Anton changed the record and began dancing around the room with Sophie.

'Are you sure this is the right thing for you?' Felix said loudly to Netta in order to be heard over the music.

'What?' Netta said bobbing about to the beat.

'Going to England. I mean, it always rains there, you know, and I don't think the conditions for teachers are anywhere near as good as they are for us here.'

'And how do you know, Felix? Have you been?'

'Well, no, but we live in the most prosperous economy in Europe now. Where else in the world are you likely to get full pay for every year you're on maternity leave?'

'Well, I have no plans to be a mother yet, so that doesn't matter.'

Netta noticed Felix looked a little disappointed in her answer.

'I hear they have school all day. And they don't pay for marking.'

'I'm not sure that's true, but I'll be sure to let you know when I get there just how dreadful it is,' Netta laughed.

'My God, Felix, you're not exactly doing much to allay my fears about going.'

'I'm sorry, Net,' he laughed shyly, then returned to his default expression of severity, 'But if you have fears, maybe you should listen to them?'

'If we listened to all our fears, we'd never get out of bed in the morning. Felix, the conditions here are not so amazing. You guys will have to teach in Dortmund for the rest of your careers. The only chance Sophie and Anna have of teaching elsewhere is if they marry a teacher in another district.'

'Why would I want to leave Dortmund?' Anna piped up, sarcastically.

'Keeping teachers in one place provides stability for the community, the pupils and us,' Felix said.

To which Netta replied, 'Stability is another word for boring to me. No offense.'

'None taken,' said Felix who clearly had taken plenty.

'Oh Felix,' Netta beamed, 'Germany is so enormous I could barely hope to see it all in my lifetime. And beyond that is the whole of Europe and beyond that the world. Don't you want to try and see as much of it as possible while you still have the energy to do so?'

'But you just said yourself you can barely hope to see all of Germany. What's the point then of trying to see even more of the planet? Surely you'll live your life in a constant state of dissatisfaction.'

'Oh do stop whingeing Felix. We all know you just want Netta to stay because you're in love with her.'

Felix cheeks burned red in an instant. 'Anna!'

'Come on!' Netta jumped between her two friends, grabbing both their hands, 'Let's dance!'

But just as they began, the needle was heard to be dragged with an awful scratching sound off the vinyl. 'Would you please have the decency to keep the noise down?' It was Gerhard.

The five friends stopped dancing and felt awkward, sober and even ridiculous in the awful dourness Netta's grandfather had poured over the room. They looked at him, at each other and at the floor in turn as he glared at Netta.

'Sorry, Herr Richter,' Anton said with a conciliatory smile. 'We didn't realise the music was so loud. We'll turn it down.'

'You won't turn it down. You'll turn it off, thank you very much. You lot may have nothing better to do tomorrow than nurse a self-induced headache, but some of us do. Some of us are actually trying to change society for the better.' Then he turned on his heels and scoffed, 'Teachers, my foot!' before stomping up the stairs.

'And you wonder why I can't wait to leave this place,' Netta sneered.

'Oh dear, perhaps we should go,' Sophie offered.

'No!' Netta said. 'This is not his house. It's my parents' house. They invited us to party here. Have they come down and told us to shut up? No. So he can go and...'

'That's my girl,' Anna said raising her glass. 'I thought the old codger had retired anyway. What's he doing that's so important for the greater good tomorrow?'

'He's been in court nearly every day recently.'

'What's he done?' Anton said mischievously.

'It's not what he's done. It's what he believes others have done. He's taking members of the government to court, believe it or not, for betraying Germany in order to save themselves from the Russian labour camps during the war.'

'How do you mean?' Felix asked.

'He was captured by the Soviets at the end of the war. Sent to a labour camp in Siberia. Some of the German officers he was captured with would, according to my Opi, maltreat their own subordinates in the camps in order to curry favour with the Russians. They also swore allegiance to the Soviet Union during interrogation apparently, so they would be freed quickly. My Opi wouldn't lie about his allegiances, so he was sentenced to twenty-five years imprisonment. He served eleven.'

'Wow. Harsh,' Felix said.

'Now those officers hold positions of great responsibility in the German government. Opi thinks he can bring them to justice.'

'Good luck with that!' Anton said rolling his eyes.

'I know,' Netta said slumping into a chair. 'He's always had this superiority complex. You would think after eleven years imprisoned by the Russians he'd just want a quiet life.'

'Perhaps that's exactly why he feels compelled to take those officers to court,' Sophie said quietly. 'I mean, if you had served over a decade in prison for telling the truth when others had escaped by lying, I don't think you of all people, Netta, would let that go without a fight.'

Everyone else turned to look at Sophie, who shrugged and sipped on her beer, while Netta looked towards the stairs, lost in thought.

3

The day had finally arrived for Netta to leave for England and the car she had so enjoyed packing her friends into was now being packed with everything she thought she might need for a life in a new country – one, she was told, had a similar climate to Germany, which meant it didn't take much imagination for her to work out what she might need in terms of clothes and linen, but unfortunately that meant she would, with the autumn upon them, need a lot of both.

She had assumed her Opa was going to drive her to the train station where she would travel across Belgium with just the three cases her mother had given her, and take the ferry to England, but on the night before Netta left – the night after her little party in the cellar which had been so coldly disrupted by grandfather Richter – her grandfather Portner had called her into the kitchen and handed her the keys to the Lloyd.

'I think you need it more than I do,' Karl had said. 'Now you can take a lot more things with you too.'

'But I don't need very much. The cases will be fine.'

'That's what you think,' her Oma had said knowingly.

And it seemed Martha was right. As soon as Netta knew she had the entire backseat and the space behind it as well as the passenger seat to fill, she manged to do just that. And with Martha's suggestions for items of furniture she might need tied to the roof, Netta would have the wonderful sensation as she drove when the car teetered around corners, that Anton, Felix and Anna were in there with her, standing up and thrusting themselves out of the windows singing at bemused pedestrians, just as they used to – Sophie sitting in the middle quietly of course where her mother's old valise did now at the beginning of this new journey.

Netta had hugged her grandparents tightly after finally accepting the car keys and savoured an image of them side by side in the kitchen, beaming. She wished she had an image of her parents in a similar pose to take with her, but her mother was too busy scolding her father for taking her away from the surgery to wave Netta goodbye.

'There are patients queuing out the door, Max, and shouldn't you be doing house visits?'

'Sometimes some things are more important than Frau Beltz's varicose bloody veins,' he growled trying to keep his voice down. 'What's wrong with your eyes anyway?' he said mockingly, drawing everyone's attention their moistness.

'I was using some menthol with a patient,' Erika lied, wiping at them furiously.

Netta laughed just as her father's wink told her she should, but she couldn't help feeling this altercation was just another example of the tension between them which she had been aware of all her life; painful secrets which both had tried to keep from each other; strangers, male and female who had intruded on the home and who Netta could still recall disliking as each in turn had clearly upset either her father or her mother by their uninvited presence. Affairs, her older more cynical self had suggested, and perhaps not surprising when she considered how her parents were separated by the war for four long years and how neither knew if they would ever see each other again, but she could never be sure and didn't want to entertain the notion of her parents' infidelity as it only served to batter her faith in romance almost as much as the nuns, who had taught her as a child, had done.

Having said her goodbyes to her friends on the night of the party, only her parents and grandparents, Emilia the housekeeper and their neighbours the Lehmanns were there on the road side to see her off. She was a confident driver by now, having passed her test three years ago at seventeen, but as she got into the heavily loaded car she felt like a novice again with all those eyes on her, especially the critical gaze of Gerhard and Frieda from their window upstairs, who were so ungenerous in their farewell wishes, Netta suspected in great part because she was taking the car Gerhard so clearly coveted.

She blew kisses as the car edged slowly away under the weight of the luggage on the roof, which sagged a little under its load. And it was at this time that she was glad she had taken the time to capture in her memory her room, the cellar, the rest of the house, the garden, the street and the faces of her loved ones in the few days prior, since the chaos of leaving she had foreseen was upon her mind now, making everything a blur.

It started to rain as she drove out of Mengede towards the western border and although it made driving a little more precarious she revelled in the way it coloured this old German life a dreary grey – it made it so much easier to leave it all behind. She told herself that by the time she got to England the September sun would be shining which in turn would make the new English life so much easier to settle into.

She crossed the border into Belgium without issue, showing the border guards her ferry ticket to Dover in England and her letter from the British Council confirming her appointment as German teacher at St. Jude's Comprehensive School in Brighton – it was part of an exchange programme which meant an English teacher from the Brighton area would probably now be making his or her way in the opposite direction to a school in Dortmund.

'Poor thing!' Felix had said of such a teacher.

Netta hoped the English teacher would end up in one of the schools her friends taught at and imagined herself teaching alongside that English teacher's friends in Brighton, imagining they would be as warm and welcoming as Anna, Sophie, Anton or even Felix would be to the new English teacher in Dortmund.

The rain ceased as she waited for the ferry in Ostend and the sun even began to burn through the clouds, which pleased Netta no end, her prediction about the weather surely becoming a reality. She got out of the car and leant against it; the sounds, the smells and the warmth bringing back memories of those holidays on the north coast she used to take with her parents and her little sister Emmy.

'Come on, Papa, let's go!' She heard her own voice, or rather a higher pitched younger version of it, and felt herself yanking her father's sleeve trying to get him to hurry up and get on the ferry to the Isle of Sylt where the joy of endless beaches awaited her. She felt her father resist for a second, saw him look down at her, his face clouded as if he didn't recognise her, saw him look up at the Allied soldiers milling about and the sign in German, English and Russian which told anyone arriving by boat they were entering the British Sector.

'Papa!' she had whined, not yet at her young age able to appreciate the shellshock he was struggling with since his release from the Russian camp. But after a moment of blinking at his daughter's face, Netta saw the relief of recognition brighten his expression and he had followed her back to the car. Once on the water she had watched him breathe in the warm salty air and toast his face against the sun. Netta had copied her father then: a big breath in, eyes scrunched up against the light. Her papa had chuckled quietly to himself when he saw this, so she copied this too.

Now, sixteen years later she tilted her head to the sun and copied him again, except this time he was hundreds of miles away, somewhere on that land mass receding into the distance as the ferry took her away to a much bigger island than Sylt. The thought of the distance between them sent what felt like molten lead seeping into her stomach and her memories of holidays were suddenly of her baby sister fighting for breath on the beach and then a tortuous journey home with a small white coffin in the car where the passenger seat usually was, with a blanket over it to hide it from view and Netta being told to pretend to sleep on top if it as they passed back through the checkpoint on the dock. Transporting the dead in your own vehicle was illegal, the undertaker on the Isle of Sylt had insisted, but her father was not going to leave Emmy there until the authorities finally bothered to transport her home – God knows how long that would have taken. They just wanted her home, with her family, where she belonged.

Where she belonged.

Netta was suddenly filled with panic as the ferry ploughed on through the water regardless of its passenger's doubts. Did she belong at home with her family too? Was her father just putting on a brave face while Netta selfishly fed her wanderlust and took herself, his only surviving daughter, away from him, just as death had stolen little Emmy away? Was her mother's cantankerousness justified? Was Felix right when he had said that Netta would live her life in a constant state of dissatisfaction if she tried to feed her appetite to see a world that was too big to see in one lifetime?

4

She drove off the ferry at Dover and tried to take it all in – this is England! – whilst keeping at least one eye on the road. She marvelled at the red and cream coloured double decker buses teetering over her as she passed them, at the long stretch of town houses that towered over the seafront, and the giant white cliffs that dwarfed everything. She soon became aware of a car driving straight at her, honking its horn and, looking around, she saw all the other cars coming off the ferry were driving on the other side of the road to her. She cursed herself for being distracted and forgetting the rules were different here then she carefully edged into the correct lane trying to ignore the torrent of abuse coming from the car she had nearly driven into head on.

'Bloody Krauts!' she heard as the offended driver sped by.

Netta blamed herself for the driver's outburst and decided to get out of Dover as soon as possible, although in the sunshine it had looked like such an inviting place to stop and begin her experience of England. As she drove, her eyes were desperate to at least examine a little of this new world, but she told herself to keep them firmly on the road, at least until she got out of the town centre and onto some quieter roads. She had a map and directions to her lodgings in Brighton. She found the A20 quickly and enjoyed the space it afforded her. The road seemed to be new and hardly used – a good way to get used to driving on the left. Her stomach growled a little and she thought of the sandwiches Emilia had made for her which were sitting in a bag on top of her coat folded on the passenger seat beside her. However, she didn't want to stop as it was already late in the afternoon and she didn't want to drive in the dark – not yet. She was too nervous to even reach across and grab the bag and eat the sandwiches as she drove. She thought of all the times she had driven around Dortmund with her friends hanging out of the windows, drinking, eating, laughing, which should have distracted her no end, yet she drove with all the skill of a Grand Prix driver then. She wondered why this was so much more nerve-wracking, and the thought of her friends made her want to cry, but she told herself that was not an option now as she needed clear eyes for seeing where she was going.

After a couple of hours the road signs told her Brighton was just a few miles away and her stomach flooded with something molten again. She consulted the directions the landlord had impatiently given her over the phone and, when she looked up, found herself at the entrance to a roundabout. Her first instinct was to look left, but then she quickly corrected herself and saw to her right another vehicle already on the roundabout, but since breaking hard to stop now may well send all her luggage shooting off the roof she opted for accelerating onto the roundabout to get ahead of the other car. She needed to take the third exit and as she turned the car around the roundabout at the considerable speed she had gained now, she felt the car list, heard the awful squeak of things shifting overhead and then, for less than a second, she enjoyed a sense of relief as the car righted itself, only to realise that the car was no longer careening because its heavy load was now scattered all over the road blocking the second exit of the roundabout.

She took the third exit and stopped abruptly causing those cars behind her, which had avoided the missiles flying off her roof, to honk and gesticulate rudely as they passed. She got out of the car and ran back to the roundabout which was starting to fill with a queue of cars wanting to use the second exit. With barely a thought for the danger of cars coming in the other direction, she ran onto the road and began picking up the suitcase and its spilled contents, a box of records, which she prayed were not scratched, and a clotheshorse, dumping each on the grass verge to the accompaniment of car horns and men's voices.

'Come on, love, get on with it!'

'Learn how to tie a knot next time!'

'You're holding everyone up.'

There was even a wolf whistle from one of the drivers, which compelled Netta to straighten up, check her skirt and screech at the queue, 'Well, if one of you had the decency to get out and help, you might all be on your way sooner.'

This was met with even more honking and peals of laughter. Netta fumed as she continued to run back and forth between the verge and her spilled belongings until a police car pulled up on the verge near the front of the queue and the young constable inside jumped out chirping, 'Can I assist you, madam?'

Netta nodded and smiled gratefully as the two of them removed the last few items from the road and each time they passed each other the policeman would smile warmly at her his cheeks flushed, which Netta assumed was for a different reason than her own, furious with embarrassment. The policeman then inspected the road and waved the cars on with an air of authority which Netta could see was somewhat misplaced since the drivers had no intention of waiting for his permission to get on with their journeys.

As the traffic dissolved into its regular flow again the constable said, 'Right, madam, is that your car over there?'

Netta nodded.

'Best bring it round here, park on the verge in front of me and then we can load you up and get you on your way again, OK?'

'OK,' Netta exhaled. 'Thank you so much for your assistance, sir.'

As she spoke to him for the first time, she noticed his eyes darken and his mouth turn down. She knew her English was good, so she was as sure as she could be that his changed expression could not be because she was failing to make herself understood. Her command of English had been good since she was a child, much to the irritation of Sister Hildegarda her English teacher. Edgar, her father's best friend had studied English and coached her at home since she showed such enthusiasm for learning the language, and before long her English was far better than Sister Hildegarda's. The nun would correct Netta's homework and toss it back to her whipping her on the head with her fountain pen as she did so.

'Portner, nothing will become of you. Hallelujah! Amen,' she declared and then made the sign of the cross over the little girl.

Netta, while nursing her bruised scalp, would examine her teacher's corrections and discover those corrections to be, more often than not, incorrect. Drawing Hildegarda's attention to that right then in the class, however, would no doubt result in more corporal punishment, so she waited until she got home and then showed her father, who would promptly call Edgar and both of them would pay Sister Hildegarda a little visit, which would result, Netta heard the two men giggling afterwards, in the nun gobbling the air with a red face and resembling a giant turkey more than she already did in her habit. Part of Netta's motivation for becoming a teacher herself was to make sure there was one less teacher like Hildegarda in the profession and now as she spoke to the English policeman with great fluency she was surprised to see something of the nun's contempt in his young face.

'Well, erm, hurry up then!' he said, seemingly unable to look her in the eyes any longer. 'We can't have you parked on a roundabout like this.'

Netta hurried back to the car, a little confused. She

drove back to where the policeman stood next to her pile of rescued belongings and he helped her secure them on the roof again.

'Try driving a little slower this time,' he grumbled. 'We follow the rules in this country.'

Netta was speechless as she got into the driver's seat and was annoyed to see her hands were shaking. She burned to ask the policeman why his attitude to her had changed so suddenly and so severely. If it had been anyone else, she probably would have, but since it was someone who had the authority to deprive her of her liberty and send her back to Germany, she thought it wise to say nothing and go.

She found Bedford Street and then George Terrace off it with relative ease. She was wide-eyed at how narrow the street was and how tightly packed the three-storey terraced houses seemed to be. She managed to park almost directly outside number 11, which was just as well because it started to rain as she arrived. With her coat over her head she ran to the navy blue front door and rang the bell. As she waited for someone to answer she had the unpleasant feeling of being a child again – unpleasant because she did not have the key to this house yet, she did not have the choice to come and go as she pleased and had to wait for the grown-ups to let her in whilst the rain grew heavier.

Eventually with a squeak from the door and what Netta worried was a mouthful of mumbled expletives from him, a barrel of a man let her in.

'Hello, I am Netta Portner, the new tenant.'

'Wipe your feet then!' the man said clearing his throat, which Netta soon found to be something he did with every sentence he spoke, 'and leave your shoes there.' He pointed to a wooden rack which currently held three or four other pairs of shoes, both ladies and men's. 'This is a shoes-off household. I can't be replacing the carpet every five minutes.'

Netta was about to suggest it would be more convenient if she kept them on just while she went back and forth to the car to get her belongings, but the look on the man's face suggested otherwise. She assumed then that this man was Mr Davies the landlord, but since he didn't feel the need to introduce himself that was all Netta could do at this point: assume.

'I'll show you your flat,' he said pulling himself, huffing and puffing up the stairs to the second floor flat in the attic. 'Why couldn't you've had the ground floor one, ey?' he said and Netta's eyes widened, not just in the gloom of the landing, but with the implication that she had somehow, since she had never seen them nor been offered, had a choice about which of Mr Davies's three flats she wanted. 'Here it is.'

He swung the door open and Netta saw her new home. Somewhat tunnel-like it was a sparsely furnished living room, leading to a small single bedroom and beyond that an even smaller bathroom. The only source of natural light was a skylight in the roof which was currently spattered with rain and offering only a view of slate grey clouds.

'No pets, no bringing people back at all hours, no mess. Rent is due on the first of the month, not the second or the third, bins go out on Wednesdays. All right?'

Netta nodded, though she wasn't able to decipher everything he said, partly because his way of speaking was not quite what she was used to from the textbooks and because she was somewhat distracted by the sight of her flat.

'Where's your stuff?'

Netta looked confused.

'Your luggage. Where is it? I s'pose you got some.'

'Oh, it is in the car.'

'Well, don't park outside number 14 or Edwards'll be over here ranting and it'll be me he rants at not you so I won't be best pleased.'

'OK,' Netta said uncertainly.

'Good. Well, I'll let you settle in then,' Mr Davies said and lugged his body downstairs again as if it were a piano.

Netta stepped gingerly through the living room and into the bedroom. She perched on the bed. It sagged under her small weight and she imagined all the other people who must have slept here before her to leave the mattress so limp, and her skin crawled. She thought of her bed that only she had ever slept in in her big bedroom in her big comfortable family home in Mengede and she wanted to cry. However, she also knew that she had to get all her things inside from the car and she may well bump into Mr Davies again as she did so, not to mention any of the other tenants, and she was determined not to do it with a puffy face and bloodshot eyes.

Getting everything inside during the rain and up to the top floor would have been hard enough without having to take her shoes off every time she entered the house. Mr Davies stood sentry in the doorway of his flat on the ground floor as Netta went in and out, probably making sure she really did take her shoes off, which she had to admit she was sorely tempted not to after the first few times, and saying, 'Keep that door shut an'all. Letting all that damp air in.' And, 'Mind my wallpaper! It'll be coming out of your deposit if you scrape any of my wall with your stuff.'

When the car was empty and everything was in the flat, Netta sat down exhausted and, with her stomach rumbling, she focused on the sink in one dark corner of the living room and the camping stove which stood next to it, realising that that was her kitchen. Her heart sank, recalling the large tiled kitchen back home with the beautiful green stove where the housekeeper would cook all manner of meals, and the sturdy teak table in the dining room which could seat twelve. She gnawed on the sandwiches Emilia had prepared for her, hunched over in one of two chairs in the room, her elbows propped uncomfortably against the thin wooden arms, then finally she cried.

5

Netta by no means thought of herself as a spoilt child. The presence of a housekeeper did not mean she had no idea how to keep a house or cook a meal – in fact she was often found cooking with Emilia or helping around the house, making a point even as a child of learning such skills as she would need as an adult, as if she knew already that her wanderlust would one day lead her far from Germany (and eventually far from Europe) where she would need to know how to look after herself. So the first task Netta set herself, after drying her tears and checking her face in a mirror, was to seek out and buy some cleaning products and some provisions so she could cook herself a decent meal when the so-called kitchen was in a hygienic enough state to do so.

The clouds remained grey and unmoving but the rain had subsided so she thought she should make her move, after all tomorrow was Sunday and there would be nothing open if England was anything like Germany. In fact it was so late in the afternoon already that she wondered if there would be anything open now.

Since Mr Davies had revealed where he lived to her by coughing orders at her from his doorway as she hauled things up the stairs, she went down with her shopping bag and knocked on his door before going out. The grumbled expletives and sighing, which were his response to anything which required him to stand up and move, soon became reassuringly predictable to Netta, but on this first day as he came to his door, Netta was nervous of irritating him.

'Yes?'

'Sorry to disturb you, Mr Davies. Would you direct me to the nearest shop please?'

'Well, what kind of shops? What do you want to buy?'

She was going to say cleaning products, but thought he might take offence since presumably he thought the flat he had let her was habitable, so she opted for simply saying, 'Food. To cook.'

'Oh, well I *could* direct you to the *nearest* shop, but I'm not going to.'

'Why?' Netta said slightly confused and a little impatient.

'Coz it's rubbish. No, if you want decent stuff then you get yourself down North Street. Tesco's is all right, cheap an' that but if you want really good fruit and veg you go to Winters' Greengrocer's near Hanningtons.'

Netta mouthed each bit of information he gave her to try and lock it into her brain, but everything sounded so alien to her it was hard to remember the names.

'Hanningtons is the great big department store. Sky blue colour. You can't miss it. Do a left out of this street and a right onto St James's, then keep going straight. Ten minute walk. But you better get a move on though, they'll all be shutting soon.'

Netta thanked her landlord and hurried off, her mind a haze of new information and surprise that Mr Davies had been quite helpful. It did cross her mind to take the car since time was so limited, but the little Lloyd had proved to be a bit of a curse since she landed in the country so she decided to walk and in doing so she could get to grips with her surroundings a little more too.

Just as Mr Davies had said, within ten minutes she was in North Street staring up at the unavoidable blue façade off Hanningtons department store. It reminded her of the enormous Karstadt department store which also loomed over the end of a street in Dortmund, but its façade was far less colourful and constructed of a lot more glass in great tall imposing panels. She stared into the brightly lit windows of this English store and felt like a little girl again, recalling the time her father had taken her out of school early and drove her on his motorbike to an ice cream parlour and then on to the Karstadt for the first time where she stood agape at the fashionably dressed mannequins and the mountains of cream cakes in the windows. Once inside she felt she had entered Aladdin's cave.

'Come on,' her father had whispered, as he tended to in church, and led her towards the grocery section where Netta stepped carefully and with wonder among the towers of tins and the pyramids of fruit.

She would never condone one of her own students being taken out of school by their parents merely for a shopping trip, but she had a vague memory of her father confronting Sister Hildegarda that day about her penchant for whipping Netta on the head with her fountain pen. Since he had returned from the Soviet labour camp, her father had a very low tolerance for those who meted out corporal punishment. No matter how hard it had been for him to get to know her after returning from Siberia to discover he had a four year old daughter, that day zooming around the shops of Dortmund on his motorbike Netta remembered feeling loved by her father. He was finally going out of his way to bring her joy and she felt only a father that really loves his daughter would do that. And yet he'd never told her to this day. Never actually said, 'Netta, I love you,' so how could she possibly be sure?

She became aware of daylight fading and this helped her snap out of her reverie and look for Winters' Greengrocer's. It was indeed near the department store and she hurried in trying to browse without drawing attention to herself, but all the boxes and packets looked so different from the way they did in Germany and she had to read each one carefully to make sure she was buying the correct item. Everything was in ounces not grams, pints not litres. With fruit and vegetables she thought she was on safer ground but even the carrots looked different somehow. As she contemplated the potatoes she became aware of a young woman about her age in a bright red coat and white miniskirt looking at her. Netta suddenly felt guilty, as if she were a shoplifter, not to mention very underdressed in her beige knee-length skirt and brown coat. She walked as casually as she could away from the woman putting a tall shelf of tinned food between them. Eventually she had filled a basket with goods which she hoped were what she thought they were and took them to the counter.

As the shopkeeper rang the items through the till Netta, needing to buy some meat, said loudly and clearly, 'Can you please tell me where the nearest butt-cher is?'

The shopkeeper stopped what he was doing and screwed up his face in a mess of disdain and amusement. 'I beg your pardon?'

'Can you tell me where the nearest butt-cher is? Please.'

'Butt-cher?' the shopkeeper snickered, 'What the bleeding hell's a butt-cher when it's at home? Butt-cher, butt-cher,' he mused at the ceiling and the keen-eyed in the shop would have noticed, shortly after, the moment when he realised what Netta was trying to say, but he had no intention of admitting it yet. 'What kind of butts do you need to buy? Water butts? Rifle butts? Not cigarette butts surely!'

And then the woman in the red coat was there by Netta's side scolding the shopkeeper, 'Stop it Reg, you know she wants a butcher. You want to buy some meat, doncha, darling?'

'Yes, I want to buy some meat.'

'There, you see, she wants a butcher. It's pronounced butcher, darling, not butt-cher. Butcher, got it?

'Butcher?' Netta blushed. If only Sister Hildegarda could see her now she would be in rapture at Netta's mistake. 'OK. Thanks.'

The shopkeeper finished ringing the items through the till while cackling quietly to himself, only stopping to demand, 'Sixteen shillings and thruppence.'

'Pardon?' Netta asked. 'Sixteen shillings and…?'

'Thruppence,' the shopkeeper repeated unhelpfully.

'Three pence,' the woman in the red coat explained. 'Ooh, you're such a racialist, you, Reg.'

'How can I be a bleeding racialist? She's white, ain't she?'

'It don't matter what colour she is.'

Netta paid and the shopkeeper dropped the change into her hand. She didn't even bother to check it was correct as it would just delay her further since British currency was still somewhat confusing to her. She couldn't wait to get out of the shop and away from the conversation which she was the subject of though the woman and the shopkeeper spoke as if she wasn't even there.

Out in the street again she turned towards the flat, feeling the need to get back as soon as possible and hide away there, but she was stopped in her tracks by a voice.

'You all right, darling?'

Netta turned to see the woman in the red coat, without any shopping of her own.

'Me? Yes. I am fine thank you.'

'I knew it!'

'What?' Netta felt the blood drain from her body as if the woman had just said, 'You're under arrest.'

'I knew it when I saw you reading the labels so carefully, like. I mean who reads the labels unless you're one of them Weight Watcher loons? Nah, if you want to be like Twiggy – and let's face it, who doesn't? – all you have to do is smoke. Stops you from getting hungry. Well, it works for me, doncha think?' she said opening her coat to display her slim figure.

'Would you mind speaking a little slower please?' Netta said.

'Oh my Gawd, I'm rambling, aren't I. I tend to do that, sorry. And you don't need me rambling what with you being a foreigner an'all. You're not from round here, are you? From the continent, ey? I've travelled a bit meself and I thought you must be over from Europe, getting to grips with the place. I knew it when I saw you by the veg. I thought she looks like a pilferer or a foreigner, not that the two things aren't sometimes one and the same, but I knew you weren't a pilferer. I have a good nose for these kind of things.' The woman stopped when she noticed Netta's glazed expression. 'I'm doing it again, aren't I?'

Netta smiled.

'Fag?' she said holding out a packet of cigarettes.

Netta shook her head and noted that fag must be a local term for cigarette, as the woman lit one up.

'I'm Rita by the way.' Rita held out her hand.

'Netta. It was nice to meet you.' Netta smiled and turned in the direction of her flat again.

'Erm. Excuse me?'

Netta turned back to see Rita with her hands on her hips.

'Do you want to know where the butcher is then or what?'

It was so late in the afternoon when Rita and Netta arrived at the butcher's that much of the meat had been sold. However, both the butcher and Rita advised Netta that a few pounds of mutton would 'do her very well.' Netta had no idea what mutton was and she was too embarrassed to ask, but in the spirit of adventure in this strange new world she agreed to buy some.

'Have you got any lard?' Rita said as they left the butcher's.

'Lard?' Netta asked.

'You'll need it to cook with,' she said and insisted they, 'pop back in Winters' to get some.'

'Now, where do you live?' Rita asked, lard in hand, when they were back out on the street.

'George Terrace.'

'Just off Bedford Street?'

Netta nodded.

'I know it.' Rita trotted off with the mutton and lard giving Netta a chance to admire her white knee high boots, before she turned around and said, 'Come on then! I'll give you a hand carrying this lot.'

Netta felt both grateful and irritated at the same time. She had planned to get back to the flat, scrub it clean and cook some food, hiding away from the world until tomorrow when she might feel more ready to meet new people, and yet here was this Rita woman, inviting herself into Netta's life before she was ready.

As they walked, Rita asked, 'So are you Jewish then?'

'Pardon?'

'Jewish. Are you Jewish? People always think I am too. On account of the black frizzy hair and the nose apparently, cheeky sods. And coz I work with a load of them. But I'm not.'

'What do you do?' Netta asked confidently, grateful to have found a subject she could converse about with ease.

Rita drew on her cigarette. 'I work in the rag trade, darling.' Netta's confidence ebbed again, but Rita checked herself and clarified, 'Clothes. Fashion. I work for Flashman's Fashion House in London. Ladies coats mostly.'

'Is this from Flashman's Fashion House?' Netta said gesturing towards Rita's coat.

'This old thing? Nah. But we do some similar things these days. Got to move with the times, aincha? I tell Henry and Zelda – they're the Flashmans – I tell them they need to keep up with the trends, but they're a bit set in their ways. Lovely people, mind. And they take me all over the world with them on buying trips. Paris, Milan, you name it…'

Netta's interest was piqued as Rita spoke of all the places she had travelled too; places that Netta dreamed about seeing too.

'… and they take me to these Jewish restaurants where

you're not allowed to eat beef and milk at the same time. So I know all about your ways and I thought that might be why you were checking the labels in Winters'. Checking it was kosher, like.'

'Oh, I am not Jewish,' Netta smiled.

'You're not? Well, that shouldn't surprise me really, what with the blonde hair and the blue eyes. So let me guess. Russian?'

Netta shook her head, enjoying the game.

'Swiss?'

'No.'

'You ain't Italian or French, I can tell that much.'

'Correct.'

'Nope. Put me out of my misery, go on. Tell me!'

'I am from West Germany.'

As soon as she said the words, Netta saw a look pass over Rita's face that was reminiscent of the expression that had passed over the policeman's face when she had first spoke to him.

'You're German?'

Netta nodded.

Rita drew long and hard on her cigarette. 'Well I never!' For the first time Rita seemed to lose some of her considerable confidence. 'Silly me. For not knowing, like.'

Netta had the feeling Rita had lost interest in her since she'd revealed her nationality. She was, of course, not ignorant of recent history and the strain the two World Wars had put on relations between Netta's country and Rita's, but Netta refused to believe that the British people – especially those who, like her, were born after the war – would somehow hold her responsible for Adolf Hitler's regime. That would be nonsensical, wouldn't it? Nevertheless, if this woman was as narrow minded as the shopkeeper at Winters', the policeman at the roundabout or the driver in Dover, then she was glad to be rid of her and she could get on with her cleaning and cooking in peace.

'This is my flat.' She held out a hand for the meat and lard. 'It was nice to meet you.'

'There you go again. It was nice to meet you. It was nice to meet you. Anyone would think you're trying to get rid of me or something.'

Netta hesitated, her hand flapping by her side now, unsure how to proceed since Rita was not giving up the bag of meat.

'Ainchoo going to invite me in? You'll be needing some help with that mutton I'm guessing,' Rita grinned so widely, that Netta found herself smiling broadly too.

Netta hurried Rita upstairs to her flat unsure whether this time on a Saturday evening constituted 'all hours' as far as Mr Davies was concerned. Once safely inside Netta showed Rita the kitchen area and explained that its condition was nothing to do with her, to which Rita's only response was to hang her red coat on the back of the chair Netta had sobbed in earlier and ask her if she had any marigolds. When they had established that marigolds were gloves for cleaning with and that Netta did indeed have some they both began cleaning the sink and surrounding area with great gusto. This chore, which Netta had not been looking forward to, suddenly seemed far less unsavoury when tackled alongside her new friend, in fact it was fast becoming enjoyable.

When the area was in a condition both felt was almost fit for purpose, Rita showed Netta how to cook the mutton by boiling it in water with some sliced carrots and cabbage, onion and potato, then every so often skimming off the revolting looking scum which floated up to the surface of the water.

'Don't worry, darling,' Rita chirped as Netta watched her flick the scum into Netta's clean sink, 'it tastes better than it looks.'

It didn't. Not to Netta anyway. Although Rita had continued to scrape off the fat from the top of the bubbling broth until there appeared to be none left, Netta couldn't get the image of it out of her mind and perhaps that was why, as she ate, she felt like her tongue and the roof of her mouth were covered in a layer of grease. She nibbled politely at the meal, but was sure if she ate too much she would vomit. Rita on the other hand seemed to devour her small plate of stew in no time.

'Have some more!' Netta said, her desire to get rid of the mountain of stew left over disguised as generosity.

'No thanks. I want to still be able to get into this skirt tomorrow,' Rita giggled.

Netta took her plate and put it in the sink while Rita looked around the flat and said to herself, 'Well, this is not quite what I had planned for my Saturday night.'

Netta overheard and, surprised at her own disappointment at hearing this, she said, keeping her face to the wall as she washed Rita's plate, 'You must go if you need to. I'm sure you have somewhere better to be.'

'Oh no. Well. Yeah, but… I mean, I had planned to go down The Studio.'

'What's that?'

'The Studio? Does about the only decent rock 'n' roll night in town. Dancing. With a DJ and everything. 'Ere, why don't you come with me?'

Netta turned back to Rita excited at the prospect and yet nervous enough to start imagining all the excuses why she couldn't go out tonight.

'I would like to but I have so much unpacking and cleaning still to do.'

'You can do that tomorrow. What else are Sundays good for?'

Netta laughed weakly and added, 'I have to prepare for my new job on Monday.'

'Well you can do that tomorrow too, carncha? I mean what on earth do you need to prepare anyway? What job is it that needs so much preparation?'

'I'm a teacher at St. Jude's.'

'The old comprehensive school?'

Netta nodded proudly. 'Do you know it?'

'Well, I never went there, but I used to hang around outside there a lot when I was a girl, waiting for all the older boys to come out so's I could make them take me out.' Rita sat back in the chair and appeared to admire Netta. 'A teacher, ey? What you teaching?'

'German.'

'Ask a silly question.'

'And it has been a tiring day. So perhaps we can go next week to the… Studio?'

Rita considered this for a moment and she searched Netta's face as she decided how far to push the issue. Then she stood up and said, 'OK. But I'll hold you to that. Next week we're going out on the town. No excuses.'

Netta nodded and felt surprisingly near to tears as Rita hugged her then opened the door, but her emotions quickly shifted to alarm as she saw Mr Davies standing on the landing.

'What did I say about having people over at all hours? And to top it all she's got her bloody great clodhoppers on ruining my carpets.'

Netta tried to find a response, but her mouth just opened and closed soundlessly. However, Rita was, as ever, quick to respond.

'Oi, you! Firstly I hardly think eight o'clock on a Saturday night constitutes all hours and more importantly these are not bloody clodhoppers, these are genuine Courrèges if you don't mind and I wouldn't walk in my stockinged feet on your disgusting carpets for fear of catching something. When was the last time you gave them a good shampoo, ey?'

It was Mr Davies's turn to search for words now, but all he found were a series of phlegmy coughs as Rita trotted off downstairs and Netta followed her, pretending she was showing her out of the house leaving Mr Davies to examine his carpet and mutter to himself about their condition. 'How dare she call them disgusting? There's nothing wrong with my carpets, is there? I'm always hoovering, well, when I've got the energy to get the bloody thing all the way up here...'

Netta waved goodbye to Rita and lingered on the street for a while in the hope that Mr Davies would be out of the way by the time she returned to her flat. As she waited in the autumn evening light, she heard a shrill Disney tune, a wobbly whistling, coming from Bedford Street then she watched as a blue van with *Tonibell* emblazoned on the side came lumbering down the terrace and the quiet road was suddenly alive with children who seemed to catapult from each previously tomb-like front door. Netta was fascinated to see the children come away from the van, which had parked nearby, with tall curls of velvety looking ice cream teetering atop golden wafer cones. She was keen to try one – if they tasted as good as they looked then they would surely take away the awful oily film the mutton had coated the inside of her mouth with. She quickly scanned the window next to the serving hatch where a pictorial menu had been conveniently placed for the young and perhaps, she imagined, for the foreign and when it was her turn she pointed mutely to one of the images.

'A cornet, love?' said the ice cream man, leaning out of his widow to look at where Netta was pointing.

Netta nodded, paid eight pence and leant on Mr Davies's wall, which she hoped would be allowed, at least by tenants, as she tasted the confectionary sculpture in her hand. It was divine. Like no ice cream she'd ever tasted before, but the texture reminded her of the cream in a sumptuous Black Forest gateau you could buy from the Karstadt, something she had indulged in on many an occasion ever since her father first took her there that day after school. And delivered to your doorstep in a singing blue tank too! Netta smiled to herself and wiped her lips. Perhaps things were not going to be so bad around here after all.

6

The next day passed in a haze of more cleaning and unpacking for Netta beneath the skylight which only showed her grey clouds and spots of rain. She thought of Felix and how smug he would be to know how dull the weather had been since she'd arrived, and when she thought of her friends and her family at home in Mengede she visualised them basking in sunshine, even though Mengede was infamous for the constant yellow smog which hung over it from the booming steel works nearby, a smog which had given Netta breathing problems for most of her childhood and which had almost certainly killed her baby sister Emmy.

She was excited to start her new job the next day, but was glad it was the start of a new term and a new school year, so that she wouldn't be the only one dealing with great changes. There would be a whole year of pupils who were new to the school, perhaps even other new teachers apart from herself and everyone would be getting to grips with their new timetables, all of which gave her some solace as she looked up through the skylight and felt the clouds bearing down on her as if they were made of lead.

She drove to school on Monday morning because it was on the other side of town nearer to Hove and was pleased to see it was an old red brick building in the fashion of some of the oldest surviving universities in Germany. The school she taught at in Germany, like most around the country, was a new and relatively ugly building, since most of the older schools had been destroyed by the Allied bombing campaigns during the war.

She reported to the headmaster, Mr Johnson, straight away in order to introduce herself and receive some kind of orientation but he seemed more concerned with adjusting his black gown over his tweed suit then combing his greying hair in preparation for the school assembly which, Netta soon discovered, started each school day. As he combed, Netta noticed a flurry of dandruff settling on his shoulders, stark against the blackness of the gown, and she agonised over whether to point it out or not until he barked, 'Come on then, follow me!' wrapping his suit jacket over his protruding belly and marching out of his study at a speed that was designed, Netta was convinced, to ensure his gown wafted after him like the cape of a superhero.

The headmaster's study was situated at the end of a windowless corridor which led to the foyer. Beyond that was the school hall now packed with students all murmuring with anticipation so that, as Netta approached, she had the impression she was approaching a hive that could erupt with angry bees at any moment if you didn't know how to handle it properly. Outside in the foyer all the other teachers had gathered, all men except for two women, and all in their black gowns too, who, on seeing Mr Johnson approach, began to arrange themselves into a line, which Netta supposed indicated the hierarchy as the headmaster took himself to the front of the line and said to Netta, 'You tag on the end there, next to Mr Moxley.'

Netta did as she was told and was greeted by the sharp but smiling features of the diminutive teacher she had to presume was, until she arrived, the bottom of the heap. 'Hello. James Moxley, nice to meet you.'

She shook his hand. 'Netta Portner, the new German teacher.'

'Oh marvellous. I'm French. Well, I'm not actually French, obviously, but I meant to say I *teach* French.'

His awkwardness emboldened Netta and she said, 'Well, I'm German and I mean I am actually German.'

'Oh lovely. And where in Germany are you from?'

'Dortmund in the West of West Germany.'

'Oh splendid and—'

Moxley was silenced by the teacher in front of him who swatted him and pointed at the headmaster. Johnson, who stood with a Bible under his arm as if it were a riding crop, was looking down his nose at his entourage waiting for a sign that they were all ready to go and look down their own noses at the assembled children and thus scrutinise them for signs of inappropriate behaviour. Johnson marched into the hall and onto the stage where two rows of chairs had been placed next to the grand piano. The humming pupils jumped to their feet as he entered and fell gravely silent. The headmaster stood at the lectern while the rest of the teachers filed into their seats. It was as Moxley took the last free seat that Netta realised there were not enough seats for her and she was left floundering on the stage in front of the entire school. Sniggers and Moxley's whispered apologies soon grabbed Johnson's attention and he turned and glared at Netta as if, by standing, she was trying to upstage him somehow when all she really wanted was for the trapdoor, usually reserved for the appearance of a witch or a nymph in the Christmas Shakespeare production, to open up and swallow her.

After an excruciating few seconds that seemed like minutes, the headmaster shouted at a new pupil in the front row, 'Boy! Bring your chair up here immediately!' As the reddening pupil scampered up the stairs with his chair, Johnson declared to the entire school, 'What kind of manners do we teach in this school, where we leave a lady standing like that?'

Netta quietly thanked the boy and sat next to Moxley, who himself was rather red-faced now having felt as chastised by the headmaster as the pupils had been. Netta was mortified – this wasn't the introduction to the school she had envisaged for herself, but the headmaster's apparent chivalry went some way to repairing the rather negative view she had formed of him so far.

Johnson began reading from the Bible, but he had barely finished the first verse when he became aware of the boy now crouching awkwardly in the space left by the chair he had given Netta.

'My God, boy, what is wrong with you? You don't really intend to loiter there, fidgeting like that for the entire assembly, do you?'

The boy stood up, redder than ever.

'Go and find a seat!'

The boy scurried off accompanied by a few jeers disguised as coughs from the older boys at the back of the hall and Johnson finished his reading.

'Now,' he said, 'Let us pray.'

Netta was astounded as everyone stood to recite the Lord's Prayer; such religious emphasis was not practised in the schools she and her friends taught at in Germany, despite it now being a Catholic stronghold. However, her thoughts were interrupted by the sight of the four legs of a chair being held aloft like antennae, edging their way from the back of the hall and causing students to bob their heads in order not have their eyes poked out by the flailing metal protrusions. The boy carrying the chair was trying to get himself and it to front of the hall again as quickly as possible to avoid any disturbance but in doing so was causing a very great disturbance indeed. So much so, in fact, that just before the headmaster got to the part about forgiving those who trespass against us he bellowed, 'For God's sake, boy, what on earth do you think you are doing?'

'I went to find a seat, sir, like you said.'

'Well, you don't bring it back here disturbing everyone in the process. Go and sit at the back!'

Netta winced as she watched the boy pause with the chair over his head for a moment just a few feet from where he had sat quite comfortably until a few minutes ago, probably, she thought, tempted to sit back there in order to put a stop quickly to the disturbance the headmaster was so livid about. However, Mr Johnson had been quite clear that the boy should go and sit at the back of the hall, so with another minute of torturous faffing and more nearly poking out of eyes of fellow students, the boy shuffled back towards the exit and finally sat under a shower of ridiculing looks from the older students sitting there.

'Mr Streeting,' said the head, 'would you please be so kind as to save us with a hymn?'

Mr Streeting, a round faced man with waves of black hair, skipped over to the grand piano and began to play while students and teachers rifled through their hymn books to find the necessary words. Netta was unprepared for what felt like a church service and so she looked over Mr Moxley's shoulder in order to at least show she was attempting to join in the singing, which was quite lusty from the adults on stage, led by Mr Johnson's belting, but not much more than a tuneless mumble from the students.

After the hymn Mr Johnson read a few notices mainly concerning how pupils should present themselves and what areas of the school were 'out of bounds' to them, together with the punishments that awaited them should they fail to adhere to the rules. Netta let out such a large exhalation when the assembly was finally dispersed that she realised she had been almost holding her breath for the duration of it.

'See the secretary for your timetable,' Johnson said to Netta as he left the stage, 'and please ask Mr Streeting to furnish you with a hymn book. Hardly setting the right example to the pupils otherwise, are we?'

Netta received her timetable and looked for her classroom using the map of the school attached to it.

'Are you all right, love?'

She looked up from the map to see a young man in a long brown coat such as a carpenter might wear. He had a pencil and pen in the breast pocket and a tape measure in his hand. Purely because he was not in a gown or a suit or a uniform, Netta found herself instantly warming to him. He seemed so much more down to earth than anyone she had met so far today, sporting a bowl haircut and small sideburns he reminded Netta of Ringo from The Beatles, and his eyes shone as if he was always smiling.

'Can I help you find your classroom?'

'Oh. Yes. Yes please. I am teaching in room L4.'

'Languages, ey?'

'Yes.'

The young man showed he was impressed then put on a comically posh accent to say, 'Well, let me escort you there, madam.'

Netta smiled and for a moment she thought he might put out his arm for her to hold as they walked, but perhaps that was more wishful thinking than reality. If he had put out his arm she would have loved to have taken it, but she knew that she could not as it would have been outrageously unprofessional of her.

'My name's Billy, by the way. I'm the caretaker here.'

'I am Netta. I teach German.'

'Ah, yeah, I thought I spotted an accent. A lovely accent, if I may say so.'

Netta glanced with pleasant surprise at Billy who winked at her and set her blushing. She was about to say something to change the subject and give herself chance to recover when they were both stopped in their tracks by a voice ricocheting off the walls of the corridor like bullets.

'Oi! You! Come here!'

Netta and Billy turned, both subconsciously expecting to be reprimanded for something, but found the object of the bawling teacher's wrath was in fact a hapless pupil who did not meet the headmaster's stipulations on attire outlined in assembly.

'Did your mother let you leave the house looking like that this morning?'

The boy shook his head.

'So why do think we will tolerate it here? Tuck your shirt in properly and do up your tie!' the teacher said roughly grabbing the boy's tie and yanking it upwards, as if he was merely straightening it for him, when clearly the aim was to choke him. 'And hurry up and get to your lesson. And that goes for all of you,' he roared at the rest of the girls and boys sauntering through the corridor, before he stalked off looking for more dishevelled children to manhandle.

'Thomas Thorpe,' Billy whispered to Netta. 'Maths. One of the old timers. I reckon he wishes he was headmaster. It killed him when Mr Shaw got deputy head.'

Netta opened her eyes wide in quiet criticism of Mr Thorpe's methods. From the parade of gowned schoolmasters into assembly, the standing to attention of the students, the religion and strict enforcement of the rules, there was a regimented atmosphere to the school which she had never witnessed in Germany. Back home the pupils didn't even wear uniform and she felt uneasy here seeing them all looking the same in their blazers with a coat of arms on the breast pocket and moving in the same way like an army of robots. She could tell she had an instant ally in Billy and as he showed her to her classroom she felt stronger than she had since she first arrived in England. Yet when he said goodbye and went about his caretaking duties she felt weaker too than she'd felt for years, a bizarre disappointment shooting through her that Billy was not coming into the class and standing by her throughout it. 'As if he would or could!' she scolded herself silently and walked into the room to find the students standing up behind their desks. She watched them for a moment, all glassy-eyed as though they each had a switch on the back of their heads that needed turning on before they came to life.

'Sit down please,' she said. They did. She pondered for a moment then added, 'And I don't think you need to stand up whenever I walk into the room. I'm not your sergeant-major.'

There were giggles from the students, who all looked at each other with a mischievous delight then Netta told them all to be quiet in German and didn't say another word in English for the next forty minutes. She enjoyed the lesson. The children were nearly all attentive, except one whom she recognised as the boy Mr Thorpe had shouted at in the corridor for looking untidy. His name was Carstairs. Eddie Carstairs. The only time he didn't fidget during the class was when he was taking a steady aim at one of the girls with the barrel of a pen which he had ingeniously converted into a blowgun, small screwed-up corners of his exercise book serving as projectiles. Rather than coming down hard on him immediately she made a mental note to keep an eye on him and anticipated marking his homework to assess his ability which she expected to find was either extremely high or extremely low. She knew his inattentiveness would be due to him struggling with the subject or finding it too easy. Either way she was determined to help him. She revelled in the renewed confidence helping others learn had always given her, but also now she revelled in the confidence speaking her own language gave her. It was then she noted how differently she had been feeling since she arrived in the country. Despite her English being good, she felt like a different person when she spoke it, with a different character and even different abilities – lesser abilities. But here in the classroom most of the kids hung on her every word and she was happy to help them improve themselves.

'Homework!' she announced at the end of the lesson.

'Mr Mobbs never gave us homework,' one of the girls boldly said.

'Well, Patricia, Mr Mobbs is not your teacher anymore

and if you want to do well in German you will need to do some homework. Don't worry! It will be fun.'

Patricia did a great pantomime of a sigh and Netta winked at her saying, 'Nice try,' to which even Patricia had to smirk.

The rest of the day's lessons passed in a similarly positive fashion. The only time she felt uneasy was when she had to take her lunch break in the staffroom. She peered through the haze of cigar and cigarette smoke and realised she was looking for Billy, but he was nowhere to be seen. Mr Moxley was on hand to talk languages, but didn't seem too impressed when Netta suggested German should be taught before French as it was easier for English children to pronounce, and the sounds bore more resemblance to the written word than French with all its silent endings and nasal phonetics. As Mr Moxley countered by describing the economy of vowel dropping and the musicality of French, Netta thought she noticed from the corner of her eye Mr Thorpe glaring at her through the smoke, but every time she turned to look at him he was marking a pile of exercise books, slashing at the pages with a red pen.

That night she went to the phone box on Bedford Street to call home, having first stepped carefully over Mr Davies who was on his hands and knees swearing constantly as he rubbed 1001 Shampoo into the hallway carpets.

The Portner's phone was downstairs in their hallway so Netta was confident either of her parents or Emilia would pick it up and not, thankfully, her Omi or Opi, who spent most of their time up in their room. When she heard her mother's voice, tears instantly pooled in her eyes, but she took deep breaths to keep her own voice steady so she could convince her mother everything was fine and she was wasn't missing home in the least. She boasted to her mother that she had been asked already by Mrs Turner, head of languages, if she would give some extra 1:1 tuition in German to a student whose parents had requested it, though she left the out details of the conversation that followed Netta's curiosity about why only this student should get the extra help.

'But what if more and more parents asked for 1:1 tuition for their children too? Where would it end? I only have so many free periods in the day as it is,' Netta had asked.

'Oh, it wouldn't be in your free periods, it would have to be after school. And I'm not sure many parents round here care as much about their children's education as the Cohens, unfortunately, so you don't have to fear being inundated with offers,' Mrs Turner had said with a wry smile. 'And the Cohens have been… let's say rather good for the school,' to which Netta could only assume she meant financially good. 'They both sit on the board of governors too, so it never hurts to keep them sweet.'

The senior teacher's words had left a bitter taste in Netta's mouth, but she thought it best not to rock the boat on her first day and besides the sense of pride in being asked to give the tuition was strong, not to mention the thought of the additional wages, so she began the extra lessons with Rachel Cohen on the Wednesday of that week.

When she found out that there were no additional wages for anything outside of school hours, including, as Felix had so accurately claimed, marking piles and piles of exercise books, she was not discouraged – after all, if it was money she was after she would have never left Germany and her well paid job and her affluent household. No, the desire to see the world and experience other cultures, no matter how daunting this was already proving to be, was still her primary motivation. She also found that being around the school building when most of the staff and students had gone home to be an almost magical time. After she had finished the lesson with Rachel and the girl had gone home, Netta took her time leaving, enjoying the sense of space in the previously teeming corridors and taking stock of her day and the multitude of students, so disparate under their uniforms, whose lives she had played some part in that day. And of course – though she never admitted it to herself – it was the time she was most likely to bump into Billy.

'You still here?' he said as he went from room to room making sure the windows and exterior doors were secure.

'On my way home now,' she said though it still felt strange using the word home for the pokey flat in Mr Davies's house, no matter how fresh the hallway carpets now smelled.

'Oh,' Billy said and she saw him quickly scan the corridor as if he was assessing how quickly he could complete his rounds, 'so am I. Well, I will be in about two minutes. If you can hang on I'll walk you home.'

'Oh, it's OK,' Netta said, 'I have got my car.' Even as she said the words she was already cursing herself. 'You could have left the car here for one night, you stupid girl,' she said inwardly.

'Oh. Right. Good.'

'It is quite far you see.'

'Oh, is it? Well, good job you've got the car then.' He smiled but his eyes had lost a little of their sheen. He rattled his big bunch of keys as a way of saying he had work to get on with and walked away. Netta watched him go for what seemed like many minutes, though it was only a few seconds, then:

'I could drive you home if you like,' she called after him, the shiny-floored corridor amplifying her words and making her wince.

He stopped and turned back to her, his eyes bright again. 'Two minutes,' he said hurrying off to finish locking up. 'Two minutes!'

A few more minutes than two, Billy jumped into the passenger seat of Netta's car, out of breath. 'Sorry, sorry. This place is like Fort Knox sometimes.'

'It's OK,' Netta smiled, 'no rush.'

'Oh good. I was worried you would have got bored and gone.'

'Well, that would not be very nice of me, would it?' Netta said, flush with the sense of usefulness she used to feel when driving her friends around Dortmund, albeit driving a lot slower and more carefully now on the wrong side of the road.

'No, I s'pose not,' Billy laughed. 'And I can't imagine you not being nice.'

Netta told her face to cool down, but it was no use. She was just glad they were facing the same direction and not gazing directly at each other.

'Where are we going?' she asked him.

'Ey?'

'Where do you live?'

'Oh. On York Avenue. I'll show you.'

Netta was glad she needed directions; it helped break the silences which she was sure would not have happened if they were in Germany, speaking German. She just couldn't conjure up small talk as quickly in English as she could in her own language. She hoped that would change and she felt her stomach flip as her brain went fast forwarding into a future where she and Billy were unhappily married because she was so frustrated at not being able to express herself to him in her native tongue. She quickly blinked this onslaught of imaginings from her eyes and concentrated on the present again, telling herself she hardly knew this man so why was she thinking about marriage, happy or not?

'Here we are,' he said directing her to park outside number 89, a small cottage-like home in a terrace of identical ones. 'You fancy a cuppa? A cup of tea,' he immediately corrected his slang to help her understand, but since an obsession with drinking tea was endemic in the English, Netta was already familiar, after less than a week in the country, with the term.

'Erm—'

'My old man'll be in – I mean, my dad,' Billy said as if to reassure Netta that they would be chaperoned once inside. 'It's just me and him. He's retired. Getting on a bit now.'

Netta wasn't sure that she liked the idea of someone else being in the house; she was quite hoping to have Billy all to herself, but she agreed to go in anyway.

Billy's house was old and dark and had little about it that was decorative – much like her flat until she had put her stamp on it. Billy's father was sitting in an armchair in the living room watching a cartoon on the television as they entered, Billy rushing through to the kitchen beyond to put the kettle on whilst introducing Netta and saying, 'Watching *Secret Squirrel* again, Dad?'

'I'm waiting for the news to start, aren't I, you silly sod,' he said though he kept his eyes on the screen as the secret agent squirrel battled his fat and evil archenemy Yellow Pinkie, who spoke with a German accent.

'Pleased to meet you, Mr...' Netta hesitated as she realised she didn't know Billy's surname yet.

'German.'

'Mr German?' Netta said with a short laugh at such an unusual name and delightful coincidence.

'No, you silly moo. You are German, aincha?'

Netta was a little taken aback, not just by what she was sure was rudeness, but by the accuracy of his assumption.

'Well, yes I am.'

Billy was back in the room. 'Oi, you, don't start!'

'What? I just asked a simple question.'

'Yeah, well there's no need to be rude, all right?'

'I wasn't. Bloody Mr German, as if I would be called that! I would've bloody well changed my name if I had. Could you imagine when we landed at Dunkirk my sergeant shouting out, "Oi! Mr German, do such and such!" Someone would have shot me in a heartbeat, thinking one of those bloody Nazis had infiltrated the ranks – and I wouldn't've blamed 'em neither.'

'Well, the war was over twenty years ago, Dad, and things have moved on. So should you. Come on, Netta, it's not bad outside we can have our tea in the garden.'

Netta allowed herself to be ushered through to the back of the house, but as she went she heard Billy's father pleading at him, 'Don't get involved with her, son. You don't wanoo get involved with the likes of her, trust me!'

She turned back to see Billy's father clutching him by the arm.

'Don't be so daft, Dad. They're not all Nazis you know,' Billy whispered before ripping his arm away from his father's grip and following Netta outside.

'Sorry about that,' Billy said as they sipped on their tea in what Netta could only describe as a little yard, not a garden as Billy had called it. 'I think he's losing his marbles. Going a bit mental, I mean.'

'My father fought in the Second World War too,' Netta said. 'He was an army doctor. He was captured by the Russians on the last day of the war and imprisoned in an awful labour camp in Siberia for four years. He was tortured and he was starved. When he came back he was strange. He had mood swings. He was a different man.'

'Oh.' Billy gulped down some tea. 'I'm really sorry to hear that,' and he put his hand gently on Netta's arm.

His touch was like a drug, which soothed and calmed her in an instant.

'It is not your father's fault if he behaves this way,' she said.

'Well, that's nice of you to say, but he's a silly old goat either way.'

7

On Saturday Netta was marking books when Rita arrived. She had Eddie Carstairs homework on her lap when her new friend knocked at the door. Of the ten questions she had set, Eddie had only answered three and although his grammar was pretty awful she could tell he knew the necessary vocabulary. German was not so alien to this boy, Netta thought, but she was going to have to be more imaginative about how she taught it to him if she wanted to keep him interested. She corrected the few lines he had written with a red pen to show him where he had gone wrong, if he cared to know, and when she heard the knock at the door she quickly wrote D-minus at the bottom of the page and put the book aside before answering it.

'Rita!'

'You're not going out like that, I hope,' Rita said looking Netta up and down with a critical expression.

'Going out?'

'It's Saturday. Remember? We're going down The Studio tonight. No excuses we said.'

'Oh dear. I forgot. I'm so sorry. You should have called me.'

'Well, I would've but you're not on the phone, are you,' Rita said and Netta blushed forgetting that she didn't have the luxury of a phone in the flat like she did at home in Germany. 'Never mind. Go and get dressed! We should still have time to stop by Electricity House first.'

Netta was curious about this Electricity House, but Rita said only that it was a building at the bottom of North Street and that, 'It's not about the building, it's about what goes on outside on the corner. Now, stop gassing and get on with getting ready!'

When they got to the street corner in question Netta was surprised and a little daunted to see the place swarming with teenagers and cars. All the cars had been souped up and the young men who owned them sat inside them revving the engines and trying to look like James Dean, while their mates leant on the doors and on lampposts, and the girls stood on the other side of the street, as if waiting to be asked to dance at an old fashioned tea dance, but with a road between them and the boys instead of a freshly polished dancefloor.

'What's going on?' she asked.

'It's like this every Friday and Saturday night. It's the place you come to meet your date.'

'But I don't have a date,' Netta said, suddenly anxious.

'Nor do I,' Rita grinned, 'but I've got my eye on someone.'

Netta looked across the road to where Rita was gazing at a young man on a metallic blue motor scooter, which was clearly as cared for as the cars he had parked amongst. He was dressed smartly in a V-neck sweater over his polo shirt and some straight white trousers which hovered above his polished black Chelsea boots.

'Come on!' Rita said and strutted across the street.

As they got closer Netta could focus more on the man's Beatles' haircut and his smiling eyes and she realised with horror that the man was Billy. She grabbed Rita by the sleeve of her coat and they stopped in the middle of the road.

'What's the matter?'

'Is that the boy you like? On the motorbike?'

'Him? God no. The bloke he's talking to,' Rita said lighting up a cigarette and pointing it at the man leaning on one of the cars, similarly dressed to Billy but with a parka coat of military green slung over his outfit. 'Now, come on.' She trotted off and Netta was more than happy to follow now she knew Billy was not the object of Rita's desire.

'All right, Billy?' Rita chirped with an indifferent tone as she leant on the car too.

'Hello,' Billy almost gasped the word when he saw Netta standing awkwardly beside him. 'What you doing here?'

'You know each other?' Rita said, as surprised as Billy.

'Do you know Billy?' Netta asked Rita, adding to the jumble of surprised questions.

''Course. Went to bloody school together didn't we. Our parents knew each other.'

'Our dad's served together in the war,' Billy said to Netta with raised eyebrows that were meant to remind Netta of the moment they'd shared after his father's rant the other night. 'Netta and I work together at St Jude's,' Billy added proudly.

'But you ain't no teacher, I can tell you that for sure,' Rita laughed.

'No,' Billy said, reddening a little, 'I'm the caretaker.'

'Oh, are you? I can't keep up with all the jobs you've had.'

'Yeah? Bit like you and your boyfriends. I can't keep up with all of them nei—'

Rita kicked Billy in the shin.

'Oi! You daft cow.' He was laughing, but clearly wincing with pain too.

Netta decided to change the subject. She didn't like seeing her two new friends bickering like this. 'Is that your motorbike, Billy?'

The man in the parka piped up, 'It's a scooter, not a motorbike. We're not bleeding greasers, are we?'

'We know what she meant,' Billy said protectively then stood back in order to let Netta get a good look at the scooter. 'What do you think?'

'I think it is very... handsome,' Netta smiled.

Billy's friend sniped, 'You can't call a bike handsome in English.'

'I don't think Netta was talking about the bike,' Rita

smiled mischievously and both Netta and Billy looked at the pavement as if they'd dropped something simultaneously. 'You going to introduce us to your friend then, Bill?' Rita said after she'd enjoyed the awkward silence enough.

'Oh, yeah. Terry, this is Rita and Netta. Rita, Netta, this is Terry.'

'Charmed,' Rita said, making sure she did not look in the least bit charmed.

'And what do you do?' Netta asked Terry. 'I suppose you are an English teacher.'

'You what?' Terry said, coughing cigarette smoke from his lungs.

'You seem to know so much about the language,' Netta said with a deadpan expression.

After a few moments of Terry shuffling about awkwardly, Rita and Billy both burst out laughing.

'An English teacher!' Billy laughed. 'Nice one. Our Terry's a pig farmer, aincha, mate?'

'All right,' Terry spat and Netta felt a little triumphant if slightly worried lest she had made an enemy in Terry already. However, Terry was saved from any further embarrassment by the revving of engines. 'The race is starting.'

'Race?' Netta asked Billy.

'Yeah,' he replied, 'the cars always race at this time to Crawley and back. It's pretty wild. They get up to one hundred miles an hour at Windy Corner. I usually go along with Terry in his Cortina.' He nodded at Terry who was now in the driving seat of the car he'd been leaning against. 'Why don't you come too?'

'Yeah, come on, Netta, we'll both go, it'll be fun,' Rita said, jumping in the passenger seat next to Terry. 'You and Billy can squeeze in the back together, carncha?' She winked at Netta.

'Are we going to The Studio? I would like to go there,' Netta said in the vain hope Rita had forgotten about their plan and could be jolted back to the sensible option with a mere verbal reminder.

'Yeah,' Rita squawked over the rising noise of the engines, 'we'll go there after. It's only half hour to Crawley.'

'Fifteen minutes if I have anything to do with it,' Terry shouted – this was his battle cry. He was about to move off. A decision had to be made and, since Rita was already in the car, Netta knew which way this was going to go, but she looked at Billy for one last confirmation. His eyes were shining with anticipation – anticipating the thrill of the race and the prospect of being in the back seat with Netta it seemed. She found herself giggling feverishly and allowing Billy to lead her by the hand into the back seat of the Cortina.

Netta counted five other cars as they lined up in the road, but there may have been more – it was difficult for her to focus amid the squeals and shouts from the young people inside and outside the car and the revving of the engines. She even thought she saw the faces of some of her students from St. Jude's watching her from the roadside, but perhaps that was just her new memories tumbling together as the car spun into position spinning her brain about with it.

'Isn't this a bit dangerous?' she whispered to Billy.

'Don't worry, I won't let anything happen to you,' Billy said squeezing her hand.

And then they were both flung back in their seats as Terry sped off and the street lights of Brighton went by outside like fireworks and flares. At the first roundabout they were thrown to the left so hard that Netta felt the full weight of Billy's body pressing her up against the window. Billy managed to pull his arm out from between them and wrap it around her to provide some protection from the unforgiving panels of the car door. As the road straightened out a Mini shot by them and narrowly missed a car coming the other way which hooted and flashed its headlights fecklessly. Netta was both scared and exhilarated.

'Bloody bastard! That's Alan.'

'Well, catch him up!'

'Overtake him!'

'All right, all right.'

She imagined her parents' reaction if they could see her now. They'd probably have her transported back to Germany in an instant. They'd spent *their* twenties trying to survive the war, trying to avoid dangers that were out of their control and here she was, putting herself in harm's way for fun. But it was fun! And then that memory of her father taking her out of school again, taking her out from under Sister Hildegarda's heavy hand, came rushing towards her like the white lines in the centre of the road to Crawley and she recalled the wonderful whipping of the wind in her face as she sat in front of her father on his motorbike, encased in his arms, as she was now in Billy's, as her father steered out of the school grounds and hurtled off through the streets of Dortmund, going recklessly fast on purpose every so often because it made Netta squeal with joy every time he accelerated.

They were swinging round the roundabout in Crawley in no time and were almost pushed off the road by another Cortina overtaking them on the inside.

'Crowe, you tosser!' Terry bellowed at the other car which he tailgated closely as they headed back towards the coast.

'Oi, mate, ladies present!' Billy said supressing a grin.

As they zoomed over another roundabout Netta had visions of the policeman who had helped her pick up her luggage from the road when it had fallen off the roof of her car last week and she said, 'What if the police see us? Won't we be arrested?' And she wondered how she would explain that to both her new employer and her parents.

'They'll have to catch us first,' Terry said overtaking the

Mini, just as the other Cortina had done a few seconds before. 'Eat my dust, Alan!'

Back in town, a few pedestrians and other cars very nearly became casualties of the race and then Netta wanted this reckless game to be over, but when Terry skidded to a halt outside Electricity House again in second place to Dave Crowe's Lotus Cortina, given the opportunity Netta would have got back in the car immediately to race again in the hope of coming in first next time. She was tingling with adrenaline and chattering loudly with Rita and Billy and Terry all the way to The Studio where they guzzled beer and danced with an energy Netta didn't know she had.

As they took a break from dancing to smoke and eat salt 'n' shake crisps, Billy asked Netta, 'Will you come down the seafront with me tomorrow?'

'Tomorrow? Sunday?'

'Yeah. Not Sunday night. During the day. We all meet about eleven and go down the beach. They'll be loads of us. It'll be great.'

'Who are you meeting?' Netta said, partly worrying about meeting more new people and partly worrying how she would get all her marking done if she spent Sunday with Billy.

The beach was a sea of military green parkas, just like Terry had worn the night before. Billy was wearing one too today as they drove on his scooter the short distance from his house to the seafront. Riding pillion Netta could examine the back of his parka which had *Brighton Mods* and the British flag emblazoned across it.

'Bloody hell. There's more than I expected,' Billy said over his shoulder and Netta held onto his waist a little tighter as they rode past hundreds of other scooters similar to the one they were on. 'It'll be a nightmare to park.'

'We could have walked. It's not far,' Netta said.

'What?' Billy laughed. 'It cost me half a crown per

square inch to have these mirrors and spotlights chromed – I'm going to make damn sure everybody sees them.'

Netta had wondered why there were so many mirrors and lights on such a small vehicle, but as they passed others with even more she gathered it was some kind of status symbol. They found a space to park beyond the pier and began to walk back along the promenade.

'Terry and Rita will be in that lot somewhere. Keep your eyes peeled,' Billy said bouncing eagerly along just ahead of Netta, like a little boy.

Netta looked at the mass of khaki and bowl-cut hairdos wondering how they would ever find Terry among them.

'Why do you wear this coat?' Netta asked trying to keep up with Billy.

'It's a bit chilly today, innit, and it helps to keep this clobber clean when you're on the bike.'

Netta guessed from the gesture he made to his pale grey mohair suit that clobber meant clothes, but that wasn't what she meant when she asked why, so she clarified. 'I mean, why do you all wear the same thing?'

'Coz...'

She could see him mulling this over for a moment, but he seemed more interested in scanning the crowds on the beach. For Netta there was something menacing about the crowds, something terribly homogenised. The khaki colours made her think of the Allied soldiers she used to see patrolling the streets of occupied Germany when she was a little girl and the sense of uniform made her think of St Jude's and the students tramping the corridors in their identical blazers, being shouted into line by the likes of Thomas Thorpe. Most of these young people on the beach were old enough to have left school, Netta supposed; school where they'd spent all the time cursing their uniform and longing to be free of it so they could express themselves however they wanted, only to find a new uniform to wear as an adult.

'Coz...' Billy had no answer for her. Instead he started waving his arms about and shouting, 'Tel! Tel!'

Terry and Rita started waving back from the beach near the pier, Rita's red coat suddenly standing out to Netta like a lifebuoy. They congregated on the promenade where Terry reckoned his stomach thought his throat had been cut, while Billy said his mouth was like Ghandi's flip-flop, which Netta soon worked out meant Terry was very hungry and Billy thirsty, so they went onto the pier to get some fish and chips and a cup of tea.

Fish and chips eaten from old newspaper was another new experience for Netta which she did her best to be enthusiastic about, but as she watched headlines about Australian forces fighting in Vietnam soaking up the grease from the food, she wondered if there were any British dishes that didn't involve gallons of melted fat.

As they stood around eating, Billy and Terry would greet other people from their 'army' and Netta was aware of the disapproving looks from day-trippers who sat under the shelters on the pier – old ladies in their tea-cosy hats and pointed sunglasses and their husbands in loose fitting suits which didn't hug the body in the way Billy's and his friends' did.

'Ought to be ashamed of themselves,' she heard one of the women grumble and she wondered who exactly the old lady was talking about and what they had done to deserve her contempt.

Netta tried to keep up with the conversations spattered with slang going on all around her, but she was distracted by the sight of the crowd down on the beach and the sound of the sea trying to hush the chattering people and the seagulls shrieking overhead, as if to try and disperse them, and The Kinks and the Rolling Stones blasting from transistor radios strapped to the back of scooters or at the feet of groups along the shingled shore.

'Oi, Langley! Who's the bird?' someone was asking Billy.

'This is Netta,' Billy announced to the short lad with albino white hair and his mates.

'Funny name, innit?'

'She's from Germany,' Billy explained proudly.

'Oh Germany, ey?' the white haired lad guffawed. 'Surprise you've got the front to show your face round here.' And he began to sing, '4-2, 4-2, 4-2, 4-2!'

His mates joined in without really knowing why they were singing the World Cup final score, but it clearly didn't matter to them why, it just mattered that they were part of the country that had scored the four. Even Terry had joined in.

Netta looked to Billy for that protective arm or those kind words she had come to expect from him and instead found him smiling at the floor without an ounce of mirth in his eyes and shifting about awkwardly, drawing hard on his cigarette. Rita, however, had no such trouble finding something to say.

'Oi, you bleeding apes. Shut your faces!' she screeched, whacking Terry on the arm.

'All right!' Terry moaned, 'Who rattled your cage?'

'You did,' Rita snarled at him, 'when you had a go at my mate.'

'We're just celebrating a win,' the white-haired lad laughed at Rita. 'We won the footy, just like we won the war.' Then he turned to Netta and hissed, 'It must be tough being on the losing side all the time, ey, love.'

'*You* won the footy? *You* won the war?' Rita sneered, 'I don't think *you* had anything to do with either, mate. You clearly couldn't fight your way out of a paper bag and as for kicking a football, well I'm sure my granny could kick harder – and she's got a wooden leg.'

Everyone in earshot laughed and jeered at the lad whose reddening face was amplified by the contrast with his white hair. Everyone except Netta. She was focused on Billy who laughed at the lad along with everyone else;

who looked like everyone else; and it was then that Netta realised he had not leapt to her defence because doing so would mean attacking one of his own tribe. Netta didn't need a man to fight her battles for her, but she was undeniably hurt that Billy had not said one word in protest of that little… And then she couldn't shake the image from her mind of her Opi's disapproving eyes that came glaring at her through the crowd.

'Ought to be ashamed of themselves.'

But she didn't think those eyes were disapproving of *her* for a change, and she suddenly felt a wave of homesickness rush over her.

'Here we go,' Terry said and nodded towards the road where row upon row of motorbikes – not scooters, Netta was sure these machines would be called motorbikes – came growling and prowling, ridden by young men in black leather jackets and jeans, many with their hair shiny with Brylcreem and styled high in a pompadour, a stark contrast to the dapper mods. There were women among this tribe too, dressed similarly and riding pillion mostly. Jeers welled up from the crowd on the beach and the collective resentment towards these 'greasers' frightened Netta. Many of the riders stuck two fingers up at their adversaries as they drove past and Netta felt and saw the horde of mods start to shift in the direction the riders were going.

'Come on,' Terry said.

'Where?' Rita said.

Terry didn't seem to know. 'Well… where them lot are going.'

'I ain't going to get in the middle of a scrap.'

'Nah, Tel, it ain't safe for the girls,' Billy said.

'You what? We can't let them off that lightly.'

'Look,' Billy pointed at the promenade where hundreds of police were amassing forming a barrier between the mods on the beach and wherever the rockers were going.

'They ain't mucking about after last year, they'll bang us up as soon as look at us.'

And yet the crowd kept moving, like the ocean, gradually eroding the coastline and Netta found they were all getting closer to the line of police whether they wanted to or not. Beyond the line she could see the petrol tanks and wing mirrors of the rockers' bikes glinting in the afternoon sun as they parked near the lawns at the end of the beach, then she heard someone saying, 'I'll give you five bob each to give me a picture worth taking. A bit of action, like.'

'Piss off!' Billy said.

'How much?' Terry asked.

'Who was that?' Netta said to Billy as they shuffled on, looking back at the man with the large camera in his hands.

'A bloody journalist, trying to encourage us to fight, so he can splash it all over tomorrow's paper.'

Just as Netta was about to say she didn't think too much encouragement would be needed, she noticed a small group of rockers slip down onto the beach and attempt to throw a couple of isolated mods into the sea. In response to this the crowd surged, but the police line moved too in order to head them off.

'Go round!' someone shouted and Netta felt the crowd split.

'Come on!' Billy said, grabbing her hand and they ran with hundreds of other mods away from the police, who were occupied with keeping the rest of their clan apart from the rockers. Their section of the mob ran out onto the road and around the back of the police line so they could charge the rockers relatively unimpeded. Deck chairs and holiday makers were scattered in all directions and Netta realised she was not running away from the fracas but straight into it.

'Billy!' she screamed over the noise of the crowds, stopping and wrenching her hand from his. 'Where are you going?'

Billy seemed stunned by Netta's reaction and the pair stood there in the road, staring at each other trying not to be knocked over by the elbows and shoulders of those stampeding around them. He seemed to be trying to process her question, find an acceptable answer to it just as he had tried and failed to find one to her question about his attire.

Three, four, five vans skidded to a halt nearby and emptied more and more policemen onto the road. This seemed to bring Billy to his senses, who grabbed Netta's hand again and shouted, 'My place.'

Outside Billy's house Netta breathlessly cried that she wanted to go home and though Billy assumed correctly she meant to her flat in George Terrace, he would have been just as right if he'd thought she meant to Mengede, West Germany.

'You can't go there now, the streets are not safe. Just stay here for an hour or two, then I'll walk you home.'

'What is *happening*?'

She looked back in the direction of the seafront and replayed the scene as they'd run away, Netta scanning the crowd behind them for Rita's red coat, but it was nowhere to be seen.

'Come inside,' Billy said, his eyes darting about at the neighbours' windows where curtains had already begun twitching, 'let me make you a cuppa.'

She allowed herself to be ushered into the house and past Billy's father who was sitting, as ever, in front of the television, a football match in full swing. Once safely in the kitchen, the kettle on, Netta asked again, 'What's happening?'

'It's just mods and rockers. It's harmless fun, most of the time.'

'People were getting hurt out there today. That wasn't harmless fun.'

'You saw that journalist. They're the ones who wind us up, the spineless bastards.'

Netta was exasperated, 'What's wrong with you people?'

'Who?'

After everything she had seen since she arrived in this country, after all the embarrassments and incidents she had endured, she was dying to say *you English*, but she knew that by doing so she would be as bad as a rocker or a mod, tarring everyone else with the same brush. Besides, no matter how disappointed she was in him, Netta didn't want to drive Billy away. And that made her even more angry; angry with herself for becoming so used to having him around after such a short time.

'If they'd fought in a real war, these kids might not be so bloody quick to go inventing one, ey, girl?' came the voice of Billy's dad from the next room as the kettle began to whistle.

Billy was about to protest, but Netta poked her head into the living room and with a smile asked, 'Can I make you a cup of tea, Mr Langley?'

'Er… Thanks… Milk and two.'

8

Eddie Carstairs, like most of the students in the class, eagerly leafed through his exercise book to find out the mark he got for his homework.

D-minus!

He flung the book across his desk and it skidded off onto the floor. Netta saw and walked over to pick it up. Usually she would have made a student behaving in such a way pick the book up for himself, but she saw an opportunity. When she crouched down to get the book she was eye to eye with Eddie and she could say quietly to him, 'Don't worry, Eddie. You will do much better next time if you make sure you answer all the questions. The ones you answered were… quite good.' She smiled warmly, but Eddie just glared and stabbed at the desk with his pen.

As she continued the lesson she noticed Eddie chewing up blotting paper until it was a sticky pulp and throwing it at the ceiling where it would stick for a while before falling onto the student sitting underneath. The harassed student would turn and strike out at Eddie or throw something if they were further away, which pleased Eddie no end.

'OK, OK!' Netta said in German telling them to pay attention: 'Passt auf!'

'Piss off?' Eddie said and his friend Peter sniggered, 'Did she just tell us to piss off?'

Netta unusually switched to English which grabbed everyone's attention, 'Right. Peter.'

Peter went pale.

'What do you want to be when you grow up?'

'A builder,' he said, slightly bemused. 'My dad says there's good money in that.'

'I do not want to know what your father wants you to

do, I want to know what you want to do. What is your dream job?'

'Oh. Musician.'

There were snorts of derision from the class, mainly from the brighter kids, which Netta silenced instantly. 'That's a great dream to have. Which instrument?'

'Guitar.'

'Good! So Peter wants to be a guitarist. Patricia?'

'A fashion designer.'

'Lovely,' Netta smiled though the vocation sent images of Rita flitting across her mind – Rita whom she hadn't seen since Sunday at the seafront.

'Rebecca?'

'Doctor.'

'Trudy?'

'Vet.'

'Richard?'

'Pilot.'

'Samuel?'

'Footballer.'

Eddie sang, 'Millwall!'

Samuel snapped, 'Shut up!'

'OK, quieten down everyone. Eddie?'

'Tiler.'

'Pardon?'

'A tiler.' It took Netta a moment to understand what he meant, so Eddie added rather impatiently, 'I want to lay tiles, on floors and walls in kitchens and bathrooms, and that.'

Sniggers, to which Netta raised a warning hand and said gently to Eddie, 'Why do you want to do that job, Eddie?'

'My dad showed me how to do it and I love it. And he said I'm good at it.'

'OK,' Netta smiled and made a note in her diary.

After school she waited in her class alone for Rachel

Cohen to arrive for her extra lesson. Rachel was late, so as she waited Netta looked over the list she had made in her diary of her fourth form class's aspirations for employment.

'How are things, Netta?' Mrs Turner, head of languages, was at the door.

'Things are good...' Netta said thoughtfully.

'Do I sense a but?'

'Well, the way children of many different abilities are all put together in one class, it seems like a bad idea.'

Mrs Turner raised her eyebrows.

Netta went on, 'The children with lower ability are struggling so they disrupt the class. The children with high ability are bored so they disrupt the class. We have to try and teach three different levels at the same time, which is of course impossible to do well. If we divided the children up into classes based on ability, then I'm sure the children would flourish in a way they are not doing now.'

'And who would be the poor teacher who got the lower set?'

'I would be happy to do it.'

Mrs Turner took a deep breath and smiled condescendingly at Netta. 'I admire your enthusiasm, I really do, Netta, but as you gain more experience you will see that you'd be just wasting your time with most of these students. Mr Johnson will not allow any disruption to the timetable like that. And I'm inclined to agree with him. Now, why don't you just run along home.'

'I'm waiting for Rachel Cohen. Extra lessons,' Netta said groggily, still trying to find her way through the fog of what her superior had just said.

'Oh, no need. That's what I came to tell you. Rachel will not be having extra lessons any longer.'

'Oh? Why not?'

'Erm... She's had enough of German, apparently. She's

not interested in learning more – more than anyone else anyway. You know these young girls. Fickle as you like.'

In her flat that night Netta sat beneath the skylight looking for answers in the inky evening clouds, until Rita appeared at her front door and Netta was suddenly more concerned with where her friend had been since Sunday morning.

'Where did *I* go? Where did *you* go? When it all kicked off Terry went straight into the thick of it. One of them rockers was about to punch me, I swear, but Terry just picked up a deck chair and walloped him with it. He went down like a sack of spuds, I tell you, the silly sod. Serves him right, an'all. And then I got my coat caught on something or someone and ripped the sleeve. Lucky I could mend it easily...'

As Rita rattled on, Netta examined her face and the bruise she had not quite successfully covered with make-up. When Rita stopped speaking to take a sip of the tea Netta had made for her, Netta took the opportunity to ask, 'So the rocker didn't punch you?'

'No, like I said, Terry got to him first.'

'So how did you get that bruise?'

Rita was suddenly lost for words, but only briefly, as her hand fluttered about her face as if her fingertips could see what Netta could. 'Oh, that? That was, erm, when I tripped as we were running away. Went straight into a bleeding lamppost, can you believe it?'

Netta couldn't. And didn't. But Rita deftly shone the spotlight back onto Netta and asked, 'So? Where did you go? I was looking for you everywhere.'

'We ran back to Billy's house.'

'Oh!' Rita sang, 'back to Billy's, ey?

'Not like that,' Netta said, but blushed anyway. 'We just hid there until things had calmed down.'

'Oh, I see,' Rita said somewhat disappointed with that

news. 'Well, if you want to know the way to a man's heart – or better still, his bed – it's a good Vesta Curry.' She shook the shopping bag she'd arrived with. 'I just bought some to make for Terry later.'

'A what?'

'Vesta Curry.' She took out the box containing sachets from her bag and Netta read the instructions on the back. 'It's posh. Feed 'em one of these and they're like putty in your hands,' Rita said before muttering what sounded to Netta like, 'at least that's what I'm hoping anyway.'

Netta handed back the ready meal, slightly baffled, and they both sipped on their tea.

'Does it happen often?'

'What?'

'The trouble between the mods and the rockers.'

'Nah. Usually only on bank holidays, but the police are wise to it now. They're taking all the fun out of it. The mods won't exist this time next year, mark my words. I know a thing or two about fashion and they'll be a new fad for kids to get into and the older generation to moan about before long.'

'Oh,' was all Netta could muster in response as her mind drifted back to Rachel Cohen.

'Penny for 'em.'

'Pardon?'

'Your thoughts. A penny for your thoughts. It's just something we say. Blimey, having you around makes me realise how much rubbish we speak.'

Netta smiled weakly and looked up at the sky.

'Well?'

'Oh. It's just something that happened in school today. I had been giving extra German tuition to a girl. She was enjoying it and doing well, I believed. We would chat in German the entire time and her conversational German was improving enormously. But today she didn't come to class and the head of languages told me Rachel was not interested in coming anymore.'

'Just like that?'

Netta nodded. 'She said she had changed her mind about improving her German. But from what I had heard, the Cohens didn't sound like the kind of parents that would indulge such a frivolous attitude to education. I've been thinking about why Rachel might have changed her mind and I remember last weekend at Electricity House, just before we raced; I was sure I saw some of my students on the corner. Perhaps she was one of them.'

'I would have thought my teachers were fab if they went racing cars on a Saturday night,' Rita countered. Then she added, 'The Cohens?'

'Do you know them?'

'No, not at all. But I can take a good guess at why they pulled her out.'

'No, the parents didn't... unless they were on the pier on Sunday. Remember all those people telling us we ought to be ashamed of ourselves, perhaps the Cohens were among them—'

'Who says the parents didn't pull her out? Have you heard it from them? You said yourself this Rachel – is it? – she was enjoying the lessons, doing well. Rachel Cohen,' Rita sighed the name and shook her head.

'I don't understand.'

'Well, the only way she could have a more Jewish name is if she'd been called Hava Nagila or something.' Rita finished her tea and put the cup on the table. 'I was on a buying trip in Paris once with the Flashmans, my bosses. And I met this boy. Roland Walzburger was his name. Gorgeous. Tall and handsome. German, like you.' Rita's eyes sparkled with the memory. 'He invited me on a skiing holiday and I told Henry and Zelda when we was out one evening at one of them kosher restaurants of theirs. Well, I couldn't believe their reaction. "We are not comfortable with you seeing him. We don't think it is a good idea for you to continue seeing him." They even hinted that my job might be on the line if I went away with him. You see, working alongside Jewish people for so long I had heard stories of the Holocaust. Bloody horrible stuff. Unforgivable stuff. But Roland had nothing to do with all that, did he?'

'So? Did you go on holiday with him?'

'Too bleeding right I did and I told Henry he could stuff his job up his backside if he didn't like it.'

'But you still work for them now.'

Rita grinned. 'Yep.' But her face soon clouded over and she said, 'And I bet you a pound to a penny that your Rachel's parents have just found out that their little princess is being taught German by a... German.'

Netta was breathless. 'Who did they think would be teaching her German?'

*

It was 4 pm and James Moxley was reading at his desk in room L1. Rachel Cohen sat before him at a desk in the front row of the class looking decidedly bored but working hard nonetheless on the page of questions set by the French teacher. Netta was passing L1 on her way home when she glanced through the glass window in the door. The sight of Rachel silently sitting there at this hour of the day made Netta's skin shrink. She watched for a few protracted seconds, then opened the door and took a few steps inside saying, 'I'm going home, Mr Moxley. Goodnight.' Moxley looked like one of the students when they were caught smoking behind the bins and Rachel looked fearful as Netta glanced over her shoulder at the German words on the page in front of her. 'And keep up the good work, Rachel, you're a very talented student,' she added in German.

'Danke schön, Frau Portner,' Rachel squeaked.

Netta kept her chin up and her eyes dry until she got all the way to the same bins the smokers used; great tall metal cylinders that were perfect to hide behind if you wanted to get your hit of nicotine or just pretend that you did to look cool, or, in Netta's case at this time on a Thursday evening, cry unseen. But she neglected to consider the caretaker doing his rounds of the building at this time of day until she heard Billy's plaintive voice.

'What's the matter, gorgeous?'

Then she wiped at her eyes furiously and tried to make herself look presentable, but it was too late. Billy had seen her looking a mess and now surely he wouldn't be interested in her anymore. But before Netta could worry any further Billy had wrapped his arms around her and pulled her close to his chest. The last time she felt this secure she was five or six years old, sitting between her father and mother singing songs around a fire they had made together while camping on the Lüneburger Heath, because then those other people, the intruders, the ones she now realised were lovers, dalliances, affairs, whatever you want to call them, were not only far away in Dortmund, but long gone from their lives, and their little family was finally allowed to heal, or attempt to heal, and bond after all the separation and dislocation of war.

'It's OK,' Billy cooed, as he felt her jerk slightly away from him.

It was a response completely at odds with that feeling of security, but whenever the shadow of those affairs scudded over her mind, it made Netta suddenly suspicious of anyone she found herself falling in love with – because she already knew she was falling in love with Billy; the way she felt so soothed by his embrace told her so.

'Why don't I take you home and you can tell me all about it when you're ready, ey?'

Netta nodded into his chest, still a little embarrassed to let him see her face. Then a thought occurred to her and she looked up. 'My home?'

'If you like,' he smiled. 'I'll even let you cook me dinner.'

She laughed and when she saw how much relief and joy her laughter gave Billy, she made herself laugh again.

'OK,' she smiled. 'Let's go.' And they drove home in her car, Netta stopping at Sainsbury's on the way to buy a Vesta Beef Curry.

9

The curry was a gelatinous faecal colour that smelt to Netta as it looked. She apologised constantly throughout the cooking process. She apologised for having to prepare a meal over the sorry looking camping stove. 'My God, the Bunsen burners in the science labs would be more effective,' she sighed, Billy hugging her waist and looking over her shoulder as she stirred the dubious looking contents of the sachet into the slowly boiling water. She apologised for having to keep milk for the tea outside the skylight on the roof, in a bag hanging from the window frame because she had no fridge, as she stood on one of the easy chairs to reach it. 'The way this weather's turning, you'd be better off storing it outside anyway,' Billy said generously. And she apologised finally for the taste of the curry, which she imagined may well be similar to raw sewage in a Calcutta cesspit if she was ever unfortunate enough to have to taste some. However, Netta marvelled as Billy devoured his plate of curry in a manner that made her think she had cooked ambrosia – by which, of course, she meant food of the gods, as opposed to that bizarre looking creamed macaroni pudding she had seen in tins on the shelves of Sainsbury's. She wondered for a moment if Billy was just wolfing down the food to be kind to her, to make her feel she had cooked something palatable when in fact she had produced something revolting which he would shortly vomit into her toilet after politely excusing himself. But he never did. He even ran his finger around the plate to get the last bit of remaining sauce from it, but stopped himself from licking his finger when he realised Netta was watching him, just in case she found such an action uncouth. And indeed she was brought up to think just that, but there was something about the idea of Billy licking his finger right then that sent Netta trembling. He washed his hands in the sink instead, as she washed the plates. She liked the way he stood right next to her and nudged her as he got in her way. She liked the way, after he had washed his hands, that he stayed where he was, watching her wash the crockery and breathing on her neck.

'Rita was right about the curry,' she smirked at the taps.

'What was that?' Billy said.

'Nothing,' she said.

As they lay in bed later, red faced, breathing deeply and grinning at the ceiling, Billy said, 'I'd love to see Germany one day. What's it like?'

'Germany?' Netta sighed, ready to feel a homesickness as she spoke, which surprisingly never came. 'Germany is vast. Beautiful cities of medieval architecture – those which the war did not destroy. Rolling hills, winding rivers, massive lakes and gorges. The Black Forest.'

'What *is* that?' Billy asked, 'A forest I know, but why black?'

'It's about two thousand square miles of mountainous woodland.'

Billy whistled in awe.

'The Romans, I think, found it to be so dense and impenetrable they called it the dark wood, or the Black Forest. My parents went to university in Freiburg on the edge of the Forest. They met there. They fell in love there. They used to skip lectures to go skiing in the mountains or take their little boat out on Lake Schluchsee.' She looked at Billy to see if he was still interested and noticed he looked as if he'd lost something. 'What's wrong?'

'Ah, you know. I just wish I could take you places like that, do all that romantic stuff, not just to my old man's shabby house or Brighton seafront for fish and bloody chips and a punch up.'

She propped herself up on one elbow and kissed him. 'I couldn't be happier, just like this.'

Billy looked at her sceptically for a moment before diving on top of her. She yelped and they tumbled across the bed together before falling out the other side onto the floor with a thump. The shock sent them into peals of laughter which were suddenly silenced by a banging on the ceiling beneath them.

'Oh no! It must be my neighbours.' Netta slapped a hand over her mouth as she giggled like one of her students.

'Sod them,' Billy grinned. 'I'll give them something to moan about,' and he hauled Netta back onto the bed.

10

Netta floated through school the next day, having almost forgotten about the Rachel Cohen situation, or at least refusing to let it intrude on her happiness on the occasions it attempted to break into her thoughts. And at four o'clock, when Billy had finished his rounds, they went together to a hardware shop in The Lanes and he helped her find some tiles, grout, a trowel and a piece of hardboard. They then drove back to the school and hid the items in Netta's classroom, making sure nobody saw them. Given Mrs Turner's complete aversion to "disrupting" the status quo and her assertion that the headmaster was equally inflexible, Netta thought it best to keep her ideas for engaging her fourth formers under wraps, at least for now, until they yielded some results – *if* they yielded some results.

The next morning she called Eddie Carstairs out to the front of the class. He huffed and slouched reluctantly to the front, assuming he would be ridiculed in front of everyone for getting the lowest mark in his homework again, something which Mr Thorpe enjoyed doing to him on a weekly basis. But as Netta brought the hardboard and tiles from the cupboard, Eddie was quite enjoying the attention of the whole class on him and pulled various faces to keep them entertained.

'Right,' Netta said as Eddie frowned at the equipment. 'Today Eddie is going to show us all how to tile this bathroom wall.' She gestured to the piece of hardboard which would be standing in for a bathroom wall. 'So you should all pay attention to him as he will be testing you after.'

She watched Eddie's eye light up.

'OK, Eddie?'

Eddie nodded enthusiastically. 'Yeah.' He wagged a finger at the class. 'And I'll be giving you homework too.' He laughed.

'Well, if you want to. You are in charge, Eddie,' Netta said and the class groaned, 'But! You must teach them in German.'

The class now bubbled with chatter. Peter jeered at his mate as Eddie deflated.

'Well, what did you expect?' Netta smiled, 'This is a German class, not woodwork. Don't worry. I know you can do it, Eddie. And I'll help you if you need it – with the vocabulary I mean, not the tiling. I'm rubbish at that.'

Eddie suppressed a smile and confidently picked up the trowel and the bag of grout.

'And Peter?'

'Miss?'

'You bring your guitar in for the next lesson please, as it will be your turn to teach the class.'

The winter term parents' evening was upon St Jude's sooner than many of its teachers were comfortable with. Like all of her colleagues, Netta sat in the hall at a table with her name and subject written on a card in front of her, feeling like the student for a change; feeling like she was just about to take an examination, except this examination was the kind where you were scrutinised by parents, who wanted to know if their little soldiers or little princesses were doing well, and if not, who was to blame?

Netta was relived to find that the first couple that sat before her seemed more nervous than she was. Peter Yates's parents just listened to what Netta said about his progress, or lack of it, nodded gratefully and moved on to the next table. Patricia Dyer's parents wanted to know why Patricia was talking about being a fashion designer in German classes. Netta explained that each student was giving a presentation on something they loved and it was helping them improve their vocabulary and conversational skills. Patricia was getting Cs only at the beginning of term. Now she was getting Bs.

'Oh, that's good, isn't it, Gerald?' Mrs Dyer said to her husband.

'Well, we don't want to be encouraging her with ideas of fashion designing,' Mr Dyer said. 'She'll be getting a proper job when she leaves school.'

Netta inwardly rolled her eyes and politely sent the Dyers on to Mr Shaw's table.

Trudy Stokes's mother didn't seem to listen to a word Netta said about her daughter, but kept looking at her watch as Netta explained that Trudy would need to work harder if she was going to stand a chance at O-level. 'Better get on,' Mrs Stokes said, 'my husband will be home from work soon, expecting his tea.'

Samuel Jenkins's parents, on the other hand, listened intently, as if they were having to work hard to understand what Netta was saying, and as they headed for Mr Shaw's table she heard Mr Jenkins say to his wife, 'She's a bloody kraut.' To which Mrs Jenkins surreptitiously but firmly backhanded him in the arm. The insult shook Netta a little and she looked up towards the glass doors with their wire mesh reinforcement within, feeling like she was in a cage until she saw Billy standing, mop in hand, smiling at her proudly through the glass. She was suddenly infused with confidence and sat up straight in order to look in control, to impress him. But as she did, she saw a man striding across the hall towards her, brandishing an orange exercise book rolled up in his fist like a truncheon, his lip curled upwards baring his teeth. He threw the book at her and it hit her in the chest. As she retrieved it from her lap she saw Eddie's name in the top right corner.

'What the hell do you call this?'

'I beg your pardon?'

'This what you call teaching, is it?'

Netta opened Eddie's exercise book, trying to keep her hands from shaking, but Mr Carstairs grabbed it from her and whipped through the pages until he found the three questions Eddie had answered the first time she had set him homework.

'What's all this?' he said stabbing at the corrections in red which marked nearly every word Eddie had written.

'They are corrections. To help Ed—'

'D-minus?' Carstairs spat. He flipped the page. 'D-minus again!' He flipped more pages. All of them blank. 'And then nothing. What have you been doing for the last six weeks?'

'Mr Carstairs, Eddie finds it difficult to learn in the way other students can, so I have been allowing him to develop—'

He muttered something which sounded to Netta like, 'Sieg bloody heil,' before raising his voice again, 'What, by tiling bits of wood?'

'Well—'

'It's no bloody wonder he's learning nothing from you. What do you lot know about teaching our children?'

'Who do you mean, *you lot?*'

'I want my son put in a different class.'

Netta's heart burned as the image of Rachel sitting in Mr Moxley's class flashed before her eyes. She wanted to stand up and scream, but instead she leant towards Eddie's father and almost hissed the words, 'That is not going to happen.'

Carstairs sat back in his chair, momentarily stunned, before he found his voice again. 'Oh, isn't it? Well, let's see what the headmaster has to say about this, shall we?'

Before Netta could respond, Mr Shaw's hand was reassuringly upon Carstairs's shoulder and he was led out into the foyer. Netta could feel every eye in the room boring into her face so, her head up, she walked out of the hall, wincing at the way her heels clip-clopped so loudly in the now silent room. She didn't know where she was going. To the toilet to regain her composure? To pursue Mr Carstairs to continue the argument? Whatever she intended to do she didn't expect to see Billy storming across the foyer wielding his mop at Mr Carstairs's back.

'Oi, you!' Billy shouted.

Just before Messrs Shaw and Carstairs turned to see who was shouting at them, Netta intercepted Billy and shoved him through the open door onto the footpath outside.

'Billy, no!' she whispered.

'I ain't gunoo let him speak to you like that.'

'It is OK. I will deal with it. If you fight with him, you will lose your job. It is nothing to do with you,' she insisted, although the thought of Billy coming to her rescue like that made her tremble with excitement very much like when she imagined him licking his finger the other day.

'If it hurts you, then it *is* to do with me.'

'This is about teaching,' Netta said quickly. 'You're just…'

'What?' Billy jerked his head back to get a good look at Netta. 'I'm just a what?'

Netta could only shake her head.

'Go on! Say it! I'm just the bloody caretaker? Just the bloody skivvy, so what do I know about teaching, ey? I see. Like that, is it? Well, excuse me, I don't want to embarrass you or nothing.' And he threw down his mop and walked off, scraping his hand through his hair as if he was trying to drag it out of his scalp.

Netta wasn't surprised to be summoned to Mr Johnson's office first thing the next morning.

'This business with Eddie Carstairs's father.'

'I can explai—'

'He seems to think you're failing the boy.'

'Eddie struggles with the subject, as he struggles with

many subjects. I was trying some different methods to get him to engage, to get all the class to engage in fact, if they have to suffer this ridiculous system of learning with peers of vastly different abilities.'

She looked up at Johnson, who was leaning on the edge of his desk in the manner of Terry leaning on his Cortina, but in a tweed suit straining at his gut and white flakes from his scalp still decorating the shoulders of his gown, the effect just wasn't as impressive. Netta hoped she hadn't gone too far and yet she was glad she hadn't been able to resist telling him what she really felt about the system he endorsed. His face gave nothing away. He said nothing, so Netta added.

'And he has begun to engage and his German is improving.'

'Where?'

'Pardon?'

Johnson reached behind him and exhibited Eddie's exercise book. 'Where is his German improving? Show me! The boy's hardly written a word since September.'

'German, like any language, is best learnt by speaking it, not writing it down, especially if you are someone like Eddie Carstairs. Do we come out of our mother's womb with pen and paper in hand? No! We listen and we learn to speak long before we can read or write.'

'OK, Miss Portner, spare me the biology lesson.' Johnson threw the book back on his desk, folded his arms and inhaled through his nose as if taking snuff. 'His father wants him taken out of your class.'

'You must not do that.'

Johnson stood up and peered down at Netta raising his voice, 'Oh, I mustn't?'

'What kind of precedent does that set? What if all the parents wanted to pick and choose the teachers their children were taught by? Where would that leave your...' she omitted the word *precious*, 'timetable?'

'Why, do you expect an avalanche of applications to leave your class from the parents of your students?'

'No, but—'

'Then removing Eddie Carstairs will not be a dangerous precedent, I think.' He took his seat behind his desk and spoke in a less commanding tone now when he said, 'You have to understand, Miss Portner, that there are many parents here who grew up during the war. Many of them lost their homes and loved ones. You can hardly be surprised that they hold something of a grudge towards the German people.'

'Oh. So this is not about my teaching ability at all. It is about Mr Carstairs's prejudice.'

Johnson grimaced, 'Oooh, I wouldn't call it prejudice.'

'Please then, what would you call it?'

'Well, let's say: an understandable aversion.'

Netta was stunned.

Johnson picked up the phone on his desk and spoke. 'Please send him in.'

Netta looked to the head for an explanation of who exactly was being sent in, but he offered none. Instead he just sat with his hands clasped together on the desk looking at Netta and trying out a variety of conciliatory expressions, one of which he settled on and used on Eddie's father as he came frowning into the study.

'Ah, Mr Carstairs, nice to see you.'

Carstairs shook Johnson's hand, still frowning and took a seat next to Netta without acknowledging her. Netta felt all the blood drain from her body and she wished more than anything for Billy to come in right now brandishing his mop and whack both these bloody men over the head with it.

'Firstly I want to apologise for yesterday's misunderstanding—'

'*I* didn't misunderstand anything,' Carstairs grumbled. 'But you can bet your life she will. Now, are you going to remove Eddie from her class or not?'

Bizarrely, Netta heard her Opi's voice then saying, 'Who is *she*? *She* is the cat's mother.' She almost burst out laughing involuntarily – and what a mirthless cackle it would have been. Until she heard Johnson.

'Yes. Of course. With immediate effect Eddie will be transferred to Mrs Turner's class for German. Mrs Turner is the head of languages and a very experienced teacher. I'm sure Eddie will do very well with her and I hope that settles the matter.'

Netta was shaking with frustration.

'Yes it does,' Carstairs said rising. 'Now, I'm late for work.'

'Of course,' Johnson offered his hand again. 'Apologies for dragging you out here this morning.'

'No, no. it had to be done, I s'pose.'

Netta was aware of Carstairs nodding briefly with stern triumph at Johnson, though she kept her eyes fixed on the wall ahead where there was a photo of the headmaster beaming at the camera as he shook hands with Princess Margaret at some occasion, though she couldn't work out what and her brain then had no capacity to try, since it was straining under the pressure of a sky full of storm clouds mushrooming from within it.

Johnson left the room briefly to see Mr Carstairs out and when he returned he was holding a newspaper; Netta could only presume in hindsight that Eddie's father had left it behind in the waiting area.

'Here.' The headmaster held out the paper for Netta who took it, still in a daze. 'This is the kind of thing half the parents that send their kids here read. It would be a good idea for you to read it too. Educate yourself in their… ways. It'll help you know what you're dealing with in future. Perhaps then we can avoid any more of these incidents.'

Netta turned the newspaper over in her hands. It was called *The Sun* and the headline on the front page read, 'THE SPY WHO BROKE OUT FROM THE SCRUBS.'

'Now you better run along or you'll be late for your classes.'

Netta was so relieved to be dismissed by Mr Johnson as she had an overwhelming desire to be sick. She hurried to the toilet in the staffroom, the staffroom being thankfully near empty at this time of day, and she purged herself of her breakfast and along with it the vile taste of her boss appeasing a bigot. She opened the small window to let some fresh air in and the smell of vomit out, and as she did so she spotted Billy at a distance walking towards the sports changing rooms, toolbox in hand. They hadn't spoken since last night at the parents' evening and, as she watched him walk away across the playing field, she felt further from home than ever.

At mid-morning break time Netta went to the room full of mops, tools, buckets and paint. This was the caretaker's room, Billy's room, and she only had to wait a few minutes before Billy returned with the toolbox she had seen him carrying earlier. He stopped in his tracks when he noticed her, but soon gathered himself and marched past her into the room, returning the toolbox to its space on the shelf.

'Can I help you, Miss Portner? Something need fixing?'

'So this is your office,' Netta said, genuinely admiring the shelves of equipment.

'It's more of a cupboard really, but that's fitting for a dumby like me, innit.'

'I'm sorry, Billy.' She put a hand on his arm and then removed it again quickly as two girls came past, rushing down the corridor giggling about something. 'I didn't mean what I said. I didn't mean anything. I was upset by that… man. And I was scared you would get into trouble. I didn't know what to say. I didn't know what I was saying.'

Billy looked so sad – an emotion she had yet to see in him – that she wanted to hug him. So she said, 'Sometimes my English is not very good and I say the wrong thing.'

'Nothing wrong with your English. That's the problem. Your English is more proper than mine.'

'Tell that to the greengrocer on North Street.'

'Ey?'

'Billy, can we meet after school? I can cook you a curry again,' she said with a seductive smile, although the thought of it almost made her want to throw up again.

'Oh. No. Sorry. I've, erm, got to go out,' he said cryptically.

'Oh. OK. Perhaps tomorrow?'

'Yeah. Perhaps.'

'What a bastard! How dare he do that!' Rita was livid as Netta recounted the events of that morning in the headmaster's office. 'He totally undermined you in front of that bloody racialist. He's probably one himself.'

'But why would he even employ me in the first place if he was?'

'Wait for me, mate,' Rita said. 'Blimey, anyone'd think you came from the North Pole not Germany the way you skate.'

They were at the Kingswest Centre and its brand new ice rink. Netta loved the sense of freedom skating gave her and the faster she went the more it felt like her troubles at school were being left behind her to perish on the frosty surface of the rink. She hurtled around the entire rink and skidded to a stop near Rita who was holding onto the side and catching her breath.

'There's a big lake on the edge of a wood near my parents' house in Mengede. It freezes solid in the winter. My friends and I couldn't wait for it to freeze over. We used to slide across it all day. When I was a kid I was racing two boys who lived on my street, Peter and Josef, and I slipped. My face hit the ice and I broke my nose.'

'Funny. It doesn't look bent,' Rita said, examining Netta's face.

'That is because my father saw me do it and came straight over and snapped it back into shape.'

'Bloody hell! That must have hurt.'

'For one second it was like being hit in the face by the ice all over again. But then the sense of relief was amazing.'

Rita didn't look convinced.

'He took me home on his back and when we got there he got two of my mother's tampons and shoved them up each of my nostrils as padding, to help it heal.'

Rita laughed, 'No way!'

'He did!'

'Wow, bloody resourceful man, your dad. Fixed you up a treat,' Rita said holding Netta by the chin and examining her nose some more.

'He had to be, after four years in the labour camp trying to help his diseased and frostbitten men with nothing more than coal dust and aspirin.'

'Coal dust?'

'Coal dust for diarrhoea. Aspirin for anaesthetic during amputations.'

'Christ! He's a bloody saint your dad.'

Netta smiled, the image of her father beaming up at her from his desk filling her field of view for a moment. Then she focused on Rita and said, 'Let's go and warm up with a coffee.'

They went out to the Lyon's tea shop nearby and as they sat hugging their coffees Netta saw Billy over the other side of the busy shop sitting in the corner with a woman.

Rita was quick to notice Netta was focused on something other than her and as Netta's face paled and drooped, Rita asked, 'What is it, darling?'

'Don't look!' Netta said putting Rita's head between hers and Billy, so Rita, of course, turned to look.

Netta was trembling at the sight of Billy – and not in a good way this time. She closed her eyes and took a few deep breaths. She wasn't sure she could handle any more drama today. She felt Rita's hand on hers and eventually opened her eyes.

'He told me he couldn't meet me tonight because he was going out.'

'Well, that was the truth by the looks of it.'

'He's with another woman, Rita. My God! I knew I had put him off when I said those things at parents' evening, but I didn't think he would find someone else so quickly. Or perhaps he has been with her all this time. Perhaps he never had any intention of—'

'Darling, darling,' Rita said softly, 'He's not with another woman.'

'Rita, I'm not blind!' Netta said and the sound of her mother's voice filled her head. A sound she had almost forgotten. Words she hadn't heard forever. 'I'm not blind!' She was four or five years old sitting at the piano trying to tap out a tune. Her mother was in the kitchen shouting at her father. 'I'm not blind,' she said. 'I see the way you look at her. Is it true? Are the rumours true? Did you know her in Russia? Is that why she's here in our house now?' Netta knew her mother was talking about Jenny, the new housekeeper but the little girl had no idea why she was shouting. She just knew she didn't like the sound so she blocked it out by hitting the piano keys harder and faster until her mother came into the room and scolded her for making a noise, ripping her hands from the keyboard and sending her off to her room.

'Christ! He's a bloody saint your dad,' Rita had said.

But, despite everything he had been through in the labour camp, Netta couldn't say that he was. And she didn't think her mother was either.

'That's his sister, Marnie.'

'Marnie?'

Netta blinked at the image of Billy and the woman in the light of this new information.

'Yeah.'

'Then why didn't he just tell me he was going to meet her?' Netta said, her paranoia still gnawing at her.

'Well, that I don't know. But looks like he's off to the lav, so why don't you go and find out?' Rita almost pushed Netta out of her chair, encouraging her to go and intercept Billy before he got to the gents.

'Hello, Billy,' Netta said as formally as she could.

'Netta!' His shock at seeing her was further fuel for Netta to justify her paranoia to herself, even though she now knew the other woman was his sister. 'What are you doing here?'

'I might ask you the same thing,' Netta said. 'Who are you with?' She asked with some warped hope that he might not say his sister and she would then be able to tell Rita she was wrong and that Billy was indeed a cheat.

'Well,' he stuttered and so Netta swelled with a sense of being on the moral high ground, of catching the little shit red-handed. 'That's my sister.'

'Oh,' Netta's paranoia deflated, but it wasn't to be beaten yet. 'Then why didn't you tell me you were going to see her?'

'Because if I'd told you, you might have wanted to come along and then I wouldn't have been able to explain why you couldn't and I might've had to lie to you or something and I didn't want to do that, Netta.' He was squirming now and Netta was sure that was because he was already lying.

'Why would you have to lie to me?'

'Because...' He leant in towards her and she had an overwhelming desire to lay her head on his chest, but she didn't. He spoke in a whisper. 'Her husband doesn't even know she's here. They're a bit hard up for cash at the moment. He's just been made redundant. She wanted to know if I could help her out. So I had some savings and well... But she'd be so embarrassed if she knew you knew.'

'She knows who I am?'

'Of course she does. I told her about you when she called.

And she wants you to come over for dinner at their place in Shoreham as soon as they're back on their feet, like.'

'Why did you tell her about me?' Even though everything he was saying was drowning out the paranoia and making her fall in love with him even more than she already did, she couldn't shake the role of interrogator – until he replied without hesitation or any inhibition even there by the toilets in the busy tea shop.

'Coz I love you and I want to tell everyone, of course.'

She was stunned. She wanted to say she loved him too, but the words, for some reason she couldn't fathom, stuck in her throat. So she looked for an excuse not to say it; a reason to be critical would do it, and since he was still shifting about uncomfortably, Netta decided that this was evidence of an insincerity in his words.

'Then why do you look like you want to run away?'

'Because I'm dying for a wee,' he smiled.

As the penny dropped, so to speak, Netta gasped joyfully, kissing him quickly on the mouth and ushering him towards the gents, ostensibly concerned for his bladder, but, more so she could be alone for a moment with the beautiful storm he'd just sparked inside her.

11

'What if a black boy asks you to dance?' Patricia was saying as Netta entered the classroom.

'There aren't any round here,' Trudy said in hushed tones, as Netta swept past pretending not to hear.

'Marjorie Ellis saw two the other day at The Orchid Ballroom.'

'Liar!'

'She did, swear on my mother's grave.'

'Your mum's not dead.'

'All right, swear on my life.'

'Gawd, I don't know then. They might smell funny.'

'And what if they try and kiss you with those massive lips?'

The girls snorted and Netta called for attention, turning to the blackboard to write some key vocabulary for today's subject of shopping on it.

'Miss, where's Eddie?' Patricia said with a smirk.

Patricia Dyer knew exactly where Eddie was. Everyone knew exactly where Eddie was. Patricia was just being provocative and Netta knew it. She stopped writing for a brief moment, just long enough to focus on the snow flurry of chalk dust settling on her sleeve, like dandruff on Mr Johnson's shoulders, but she quickly regained her composure and finished what she was writing. Then, keeping her face to the board, she bought herself a little more time by saying, 'In German please, Patricia.'

Patricia sighed, but very quickly and with much more competence than she could have at the beginning of the term said in a fine accent, 'Frau Portner, wo ist Eddie?'

Netta considered rattling off a convoluted sentence in German at great speed containing many complex words and grammatical constructions in order to bamboozle the class into silence on the subject, but her desire to help the class improve their German could never be quashed and so she said, 'Eddie's father is a bigoted fool who thinks all Germans are Nazis, so Eddie will now be taught by Mrs Turner, who seems to have no grasp of good education, at the command of Mr Johnson who is an insensitive and sycophantic arse.' At least that's what she momentarily fantasised about saying before opting for the more ambiguous: 'It has been decided that Eddie will do better in Mrs Turner's class. Now, who is going to be the shopkeeper?'

As some eager hands shot up, Netta looked through the little forest they made at the chair next to Peter which now gaped with Eddie's absence and then towards the cupboard in which stood a beautifully tiled piece of hardwood.

At the end of the lesson the students threw themselves at the exit as usual, trying to stuff each other through it like the commuters getting on the train to London, who Rita often moaned to Netta about. Before Patricia and Trudy could get through she called them back and they looked at each other guiltily before slouching over to stand before Netta's desk.

'Some black boys come from a different country. Or their parents are from a different country. Just like me. If you meet one, why don't you start by asking them all about it? And tell them about where you come from. I think both you and the black boys will find it ever so interesting.'

Patricia and Trudy looked bewildered, but nodded silently as their faces reddened rapidly. Netta sent them on their way and smiled to herself at the sound of the girls' hissed chatter which exploded from them as they left the room.

'What are you eating, Mr Langley?'

To Netta it looked like a layer of white wax over a deeper layer of Vesta Curry which he had spread on his toast.

'Toast and dripping,' he said his mouth full of irritation as well as the food.

'What is dripping?' Netta asked, but that was as much as she was going to get out of Mr Langley today. Unless he was asking for milk and two sugars in his tea he tried not to speak to Netta, unless saying something meant she might leave him in peace quickly. She turned back to the kitchen and looked to Billy for an answer instead. 'I thought dripping was the present participle, not a noun,' she said.

'Ey?'

'Dripping? On toast?'

'Oh, it's the fat from the Sunday roast left to congeal in the fridge. He swears by it,' Billy said pretending to vomit.

'My God, what is it with you British and fat?' Netta said and far from pretending to vomit she hurried to the toilet and actually did.

'Are you all right, gorgeous?' Billy's voice came from outside the toilet door.

'Yes. Better now,' Netta said quickly checking her mouth and hair in the mirror for any stray bits of puke before opening the door to show Billy she was fine. 'I've had a bug for a while now. I think it's about time I see a doctor.'

'I don't s'pose me talking about dripping helped, ey?'

Netta smiled and said, 'I can't wait to get back to some good German cooking.'

She saw Billy's brow furrow and he said, 'Are you… Are you going back?'

'Not for good,' she said quickly to ease his anxiety, 'but I thought I might go home for Christmas.'

After all the horrible experiences at school this term, Netta had been craving the familiarity of home: the people, the sights, the sounds, the tastes, especially since it was too cold now for the Tonibell ice cream man to come round with her favourite, her only, English comfort food. She didn't even know she had made the decision until that moment when Billy's question had forced her to articulate it. And just then another thought occurred to her which she articulated a lot quicker. 'Would you come with me?'

'To Germany?' Billy looked terrified and excited all at once.

'Yes. You said you wanted to see it. I'd love to show it to you. I'd love you to meet my friends. And my family,' she was almost hopping on the spot now at the thought of showing Germany off to him and Billy off to Germany.

'What, for Christmas day and everything?'

Netta nodded.

'Well,' he looked around the room and to Netta it looked as if he was looking for an excuse. He found one. 'But I have to look after Dad. He'll have no one to have his Christmas dinner with.'

'Oh. OK.' Netta said, totally deflated, but telling herself not to get annoyed at Billy. After all, how could she possibly ask Billy to leave his family for hers? If the boot was on the other foot and he asked her to stay with him and his father in this dingy place, she would struggle to accept.

The doorbell and Billy's dad swearing at it stopped any further conversation on this matter, as Billy went to answer the door and Rita burst in bringing the bright colours of her clothes and the energy of her unquenchable spirit into the drab and tired house.

'All right, Bill? All right, Albert?' she said grabbing Billy's father by the ears and kissing him on the few strands of hair combed across the bald dome of his head.

'Piss off, you!' Billy's father said, spitting bits of toast and dripping across the carpet.

'Mind out,' Rita laughed, 'you're making a mess. Where's the carpet sweeper, Bill?'

Billy dutifully brought the carpet sweeper from the cupboard under the stairs and Rita quickly used it to hoover up the few spots of food on the floor. Netta watched

Rita with awe and a certain degree of envy for the way she seemed so fearless of Mr Langley – or Albert as she now knew he was called, though she also knew she wouldn't be addressing him as such any time soon.

'All right, Nets? Blimey, you look like you lost a shilling and found sixpence.'

'My fault,' Billy said. 'She asked me to go to Germany for Christmas…'

'And?' Rita was wide-eyed with anticipation.

'Well, I can't, can I, not with him being here,' he said pointing to the back of his father's armchair.

'You what?' Rita squawked and shoved the carpet sweeper at him. 'You'd pass up a chance to go abroad with your girlfriend coz of grumpy guts here? Are you barmy?'

Billy fiddled with the handle of the sweeper, but Netta wasn't sure if his embarrassment was because of his decision or the way Rita spoke about his father who was sitting a few feet away, apparently absorbed in a quiz show on the television.

'He can come round ourn for Christmas.'

'He bloody can't,' Albert croaked, apparently not so absorbed in *Take Your Pick* after all.

'Oh shut up, you,' Rita said. 'You'll come round to ours and we'll have a right laugh. We have a full house at Christmas. You'd love it. You and my aunt Doe would get along like a house on fire.' She added in a stage whisper to Netta, 'She's a grumpy old sod, an'all.'

Netta tried to smile for Rita, but she was feeling queasy again.

'I heard that.'

'You were meant to. So that settles it.'

'No it doesn't, it settles nothing.'

Then Netta was rushing to the toilet. She vomited again and this time as she made sure she was looking presentable in the mirror she heard Albert's voice coming from the living room.

'Billy, don't go over there, son. Take it from me. Once they get you in their clutches they'll never let you go!'

'Jesus, Dad, they're not the Gestapo.'

Netta put her ear to the door. She thought she heard the sound of sobbing. 'So you're gunoo leave your old man all alone at Christmas?' Albert was clearly pulling out all the stops to prevent his son getting too close to Netta.

She opened the door so that they could hear the toilet flushing, announcing her return, saving her from walking in on any more of Albert's insults.

'Do not worry about it, Billy,' she said gloomily. 'You should stay here.'

And Billy didn't argue.

'Blimey. You poorly?' Rita said.

'Just an upset stomach.'

Rita suddenly looked panicked. 'You still up for coming down The Studio?'

Netta nodded.

Rita slapped a hand on her chest and breathed a sigh of relief. 'Oh good. Terry's waiting for us in the car. He wouldn't be happy to have driven all this way if you weren't coming.'

'He only lives down Church Road,' Billy said slamming the carpet sweeper back in the cupboard.

'I know, but it's not exactly on the way to The Studio, is it,' Rita said weakly before snapping back into her usual self, clapping her hands and saying, 'Well, chop-chop! Are you ready or what?'

'OK, Dad, we're off now.'

'Thank Gawd for that.'

'Now, no need to be rude. You got your toast and your newspaper, aincha.'

Netta's heart sank as Billy spread *The Sun* over his father's lap as one would spread a blanket over a baby.

Netta was sitting under the skylight, using every last smudge of December light to see the books she was marking before she turned on the lamp. She avoided turning on the lights in her flat for as long as possible, not only to save money (she thought of the conceited look on Felix's face when he found out she wasn't getting paid for any of this marking), but because as soon as she turned on the lights inside the flat, the world outside suddenly seemed darker and gloomier than ever. But the thought of seeing her friends and family, including Felix, next week kept her spirits up.

As she realised she had Richard Kirk's homework almost pressed to her nose in order to see it, she got up and went to flick on the light switch near the door and, as she did so, she heard a commotion on the stairs. She opened the door slightly so she could hear better and Mr Davies's ranting reached her from the floor below.

'You mind my wallpaper, you. If you take a chunk out of it, you'll be replacing the whole lot.'

'Perhaps we could replace it with something nice then,' came Billy's response, made under his breath and between clenched teeth.

Netta, still unable to see them both at this point, was suddenly scared Billy might be about to bash her landlord over the head with a mop, as he almost did Mr Carstairs, so she hurried down to the next landing to see that the main cause of Billy's clenched teeth was not in fact Mr Davies, but the refrigerator he was trying to carry by himself up the stairs.

'Billy!' she cried and rushed to help him, since, far from assisting Billy not to damage his precious walls, the harassment her landlord was giving him would only make Billy more likely to crash into them.

'And don't you drag it along them carpets. Lift it. My carpets are in pristine condition and if I see any marks...'

As Netta glanced down to see Billy's shoeless feet, she

burned to remind Mr Davies how the condition of his carpets had improved only since Rita had told him how dubious it was, but she decided to focus all her energy on helping Billy instead, as the doors to both flats on the landing opened and she saw more of her fellow tenants, as they gawped at the scene, than she had all term.

'Why don't you supply your tenants with a fridge anyway?' Billy said straining beneath the cream coloured cabinet as Netta backed up the stairs to her room, bent over like an old woman as she tried to steady it, feeling she was in fact making little difference, but determined to show Mr Davies and Billy that at least she was trying to help. 'A flat is not fit for purpose if it doesn't have a fridge these days.'

'I rent rooms, not appliances. I'm not bloody Rumbelows you know. And you'll be paying a lot more for your electricity, young lady, with that up there. Don't think I'll be footing the bill!'

It only occurred to Netta then that this fridge was for her. In all the clamour she hadn't even questioned why Billy might be lugging one up the stairs towards her flat on a Sunday evening. She had just seen him in need of help and had unquestioningly come to his aid; and the rush of warmth this action had sent through her she was thrilled to identify as love.

As the landlord ranted on as if he was choking on toast and dripping, Billy edged the fridge inside Netta's flat far enough so he could slam the door shut on Mr Davies. He then leant over the fridge, gasping for breath and laughing at Netta, who returned his laughter, though her face registered fear for her boyfriend's health after all that exertion.

'Have some water!' she insisted and quickly poured him a glass.

'Thanks, gorgeous,' he said downing the drink then adding, flicking at a small red bow stuck on the door of the fridge, 'Merry Christmas!'

Netta was so pleasantly shocked by the gift she could only manage, 'For me?'

'Well, I didn't drag it all the way up to your flat for the Queen, did I?'

'I love it.'

'Well, it's only second hand, but I've given her a good servicing and I think she'll see you all right for a bit. I know it's brass monkeys outside, but we can't have you storing your milk on the roof any longer, can we?'

'Brass monkeys?' Netta said with a baffled giggle.

'Oh sorry. It means freezing cold. Don't ask me why, but it does. Now, where shall we put it?'

'Over here? Next to the sink?'

Netta enjoyed the way they worked together to establish a place for the fridge and she was suddenly flushed with images of them setting up a home together, which made her want to grab at her chest to steady her heart. For a moment she even contemplated telling Billy she would stay with him and his father for Christmas and not go back to Germany after all, but what came out of her mouth was, 'I haven't got your present yet. I will, before I go, but school has been so busy—'

'It's OK. Take your time. You can give it to me on Christmas Day if you like.'

Netta frowned, unsure of his meaning.

'I've told Dad he's spending Christmas with Rita whether he likes it or not. I'm coming with you.' Netta saw Billy's face drop as he read her utter surprise as displeasure. 'I-I-If you still want me to, but it don't matter if you don't—'

Netta threw her arms around him and kissed him repeatedly. 'Of course I want you to.'

'Well, good!' Billy grinned. 'Coz I love you, Miss Portner.'

Netta took a sharp intake of breath as if to say something in response. And she knew the response that was expected of her. And she wanted to say the expected response. She knew she felt the expected the response – her aching heart told her so. But, as before in the tea shop, the words stuck in her throat. She buried her face in his neck and kissed him to hide her silence, hoping the gesture would be enough, but when she finally glanced at his face she saw the sad face of a child. And that child was Netta. She was four years old standing on the platform of Mengede station next to her mother and grandparents, the parents of the father she had never met. She clutched a little bunch of daffodils, a present she had picked for him, the handsome, clever-looking soldier in a smart uniform in the photograph her mother had shown her every night before bed. The pale man, whom Netta saw shuffling down the platform towards her, looked like he may be sharp to the touch for his collarbones stood out through the open neck of his shirt and his hands looked more like the skeleton's hand in her mother's medical books than those of a person with skin and muscles on top. His mangy jacket seemed to sit oddly on his frame, as if it had been made by a very bad seamstress. But nevertheless Netta knew he would sweep her up in his arms and kiss her and tell her how much he loved her, because, after all, he was her father, returned at last.

When he came to a stop in front of the family, no one seemed to know quite what to do. Netta heard her mother's voice quivering, saw her hands fluttering, as if in fear of something. Fear the man might stumble? Fear he might know about the other man who'd came to visit her; the man Netta's Oma had warned to stay away? 'Give him the flowers and say hello then!' Netta's mother said, her body inclining tentatively towards her husband, waiting for the embrace that never came.

Netta handed the man the daffodils. He handed her a round brown Bakelite tin full of sweets. That was all. There was no hug, no kisses, no 'I love you'. The sweets should have been the perfect anaesthetic to numb the little girl's disappointment, but as she walked behind him out of the station she quietly wept, deprived of the fairy-tale ending she had always dreamed of; the fairy-tale ending to those long fatherless years.

She yearned to give Billy the response he craved. Yearned to reignite his eyes with three simple words. But nothing came.

'Now,' he said, patting his pockets and looking around the room as if for the answer to his question, 'What do I need to pack for Germany? I've never been abroad except for the Isle of Wight. Does that count?'

12

etta watched Billy's face as she parked the car at the side of her family's house in Mengede. She saw his eyes widen, not because of the dark winter evening, but because he realised this expansive new place with its very own driveway and large garden behind, so unlike his own house in Brighton, was where Netta came from. When she saw him swallow hard as if he was preparing himself for a death-defying leap, Netta felt like hugging Billy and telling him not to worry, and yet at the same time she felt a buzz of pride that her home could impress him so much and that at last he was seeing that there was more to her than that pokey flat rented from a miserable landlord in a house squashed into a terrace in a southern English town – she almost felt exotic! She was about to take Billy's hand when she noticed Martha's face in the glow from the kitchen window, eager to see who was arriving, and then heard her shriek out happily to whoever else was in there with her. This caused Netta to jump out of the car, leaving Billy as she met Martha and Karl by the kitchen door, who both embraced her so warmly she thought the tears beginning to pool in her eyes might spill out if they squeezed her any harder. Then her father came from inside and greeted her too, but Netta could feel him looking over her shoulder as they embraced and she turned to follow his gaze to the car where she could see the shadow of Billy, his head nodding and his hand moving in the manner of a conductor, and she knew he was rehearsing his own greeting in German, just as he had learned it from Netta. She remembered, as she hurried to the car to get Billy now, how strange it was that he had not only had to ask her to teach him, but he had had to beg her to do so. She had said rather theatrically that she couldn't be bothered to teach him any German after teaching the subject all day at school, but that wasn't really true. Although she was tired, there were few things she loved more than imparting her knowledge of languages and seeing someone learn and, although it would have made her life so much easier if Billy was a fluent German speaker, there was something secretly desirable about keeping him ignorant of the language. She suspected deep down it was because it kept him dependent on her to a large extent here in her own country, but she had refused to articulate the notion any further. Now as Billy got out of the car and came to the kitchen door where he stood holding out his hand to her father, Netta felt her insides swirling with pride and embarrassment as he said 'Hello. Pleased to meet you,' in German worse than Eddie Carstairs's at the beginning of the autumn term.

Her father smiled politely as his eyes searched the air for a translation, so Karl broke the silence by asking Netta, 'How's the car been behaving?'

'Wonderfully, thanks, Opa,' Netta managed in response though she was fixed on the sight of Billy and her father awkwardly assessing each other as they continued to shake hands.

'Well, come in! Come in!' her father said eventually, gesticulating wildly to help Billy understand his meaning. 'It's too cold to be standing in the doorway.'

'Oh, thanks. Danke.' Billy said goofily, then stopped and asked, 'Oh... Ought we get the stuff out the car first?'

Everyone looked at Netta for a translation. Karl's English was competent, Martha's wasn't bad either, but Billy's accent and diction made his English sound like another language altogether to them.

'We should get the luggage from the car first,' Netta explained, a confidence boarding on arrogance surging through her as she not only felt all the insecurity of being among foreigners for the past few months lifting, but also realised the value of her new status in the family as the bridge between them and their alien guest. But her grand-parents wouldn't hear of it.

'Oh, do not worry,' Karl announced in English to Billy, 'We will bring the luggage. You go inside where it is warm.'

'Oh, don't mind if I do, ta very much.'

Everyone stopped and turned to Netta again.

'He said, thanks,' she said to which her grandparents snapped back into action and she followed Billy and her father inside.

'Where's Mama?' Netta asked her father as he ushered them into the living room.

'She had one last patient to attend to,' he said gesturing towards the large annex at the front of the house which formed the surgery on the ground floor and Martha and Karl's living quarters above. 'Dear Frau Beltz came without an appointment, claiming she was dying, again!'

Netta and her father laughed wryly and Billy looked up at them questioningly from the sofa where he perched. Netta was about to explain the family joke, but realised it would be lost on Billy, who, of course, didn't know Frau Beltz and her dramatic ways, so instead just said. 'My mother's just finishing work. She'll be here soon.'

'Can I get you both a coffee?' Netta's father said to her.

'Coffee?' Netta asked Billy as she hovered in the middle of the room unsure whether to sit on the sofa like a guest or go and help make the drinks as she used to when she lived here.

Billy hesitated, and Netta knew he was pondering whether to be polite and say yes or say what he really wanted. And after an excruciatingly long 'Erm…' he said, 'Actually I could kill a cuppa tea if you've got it.' Then, as he saw Max's face cloud over, he bravely tried to ask in German. 'Eine Tass du Thé,' he announced mixing in some broken French, which he had picked up as a child in school before his attention was diverted to subjects he saw as more useful and exciting, such as Woodwork and P.E.

Max stared, his mouth open slightly, as he tried to understand what had just been said.

'Eine Tasse Tee,' Netta corrected smiling reassuringly at Billy and then at her father with an expression which pleaded with him to appreciate the effort her boyfriend was making.

'Oh, tea!' Max cried. 'Yes, yes, I'm sure we could find some,' and he hurried out to the kitchen – not something he was usually quick to do, but clearly, Netta felt, he needed respite already from his efforts to surmount the language barrier.

However, his exit was blocked by Karl and Martha carrying Billy and Netta's luggage. Billy jumped up to help them set it down, despite their continued protestations.

'He wants tea. I'm just getting him tea.'

'You don't need to make tea. I'll make the tea. You stay here and chat. Netta, you don't want tea, do you?'

'No, coffee please, but I can make it.'

'No, no, sit down with your... friend and tell him to sit down to.'

''Ere you go, I'll grab that, thanks, Mrs Portner.'

'What did he say? Max, take that one from your father. You know his wrist won't be strong enough.'

'No, no, leave me alone. I'm fine, son. My God, Martha, I'm more than capable of lifting a little suitcase, you know.'

Netta wasn't sure whether to be exhausted or amused by the bundle of bodies in the doorway bickering over who was making tea and who was carrying luggage, but she had an overwhelming urge to run up to her room with Billy and hide away from it all and sleep in his arms as she did as often as possible in Brighton. She found herself turning to the door which led to the hall as if getting ready to go, but that exit too was now barred as her mother stood in it watching the commotion on the other side of the room.

'Mama!' Netta hugged her mother, who returned the embrace warmly enough, but then quickly held her daughter by the shoulders and examined her face with the kind of clinical detachment with which she had examined patients all day. However, this examination had the added scrutiny that only a mother can conjure of her child. Netta felt, as her mother pressed her thumbs on her cheeks to open Netta's eyes wide, that her mother was looking not only at her pupils but beyond them into her very soul, her memories even, and so she tried desperately to banish any of those thoughts of herself in bed with Billy.

'How are you?' her mother asked at last, her voice serrated with suspicion.

'Fine!' Netta insisted, breaking away and introducing Billy to her, who now stood in the middle of the living room with Max, both men deprived of a job, as Karl disappeared upstairs with their cases.

'Have you been sick?' Erika said after a brief and rather cold hello to Billy.

Netta sighed, 'I had a bit of a stomach bug for a while, I think, but it's fine now.'

'What made you sick?'

'I don't know, Mama. Probably some of the food. You should see some of the terrible things they eat over there.'

'Well, you can't let your health suffer by eating poorly.'

'It's just a matter of adjusting and working out what's good to eat, that's all.'

Erika didn't look convinced and jutted her chin in Billy's direction saying, 'And where did you meet him? At the school?'

'Yes. I told you on the phone.'

'So he's a teacher too?'

'No, Mama, I told you that too,' Netta said falling back into her role of exasperated teenager, which her mother could so easily bring out of her. 'He's in charge of the maintenance of the building.'

'A caretaker?' Erika said snootily.

'Yes,' Netta said finding Billy's hand, 'and a very good one.'

'Everything OK?' Billy said with some apprehension trying to use the expressions on the two women's faces to translate their words.

'Yes, I was just explaining to Mama how we met and how good you are at your job.'

Billy laughed shyly. 'Well, I don't know about that.'

Netta felt the need to change the subject and found an opportunity in the small wooden crib on the window sill, which had been placed there at the beginning of every advent she could remember.

'I see you're still putting the crib out.'

'Why not?' her mother said, blushing slightly. 'Traditions are important.'

'You even have the hay and the straw,' Netta said going to the window and fingering the two little piles either side of the crib. 'Billy.'

Billy came over eagerly, glad to have Netta to talk to in English.

'When I was a child, every night during advent, I had to choose some hay to put into the crib if I had been good, or some straw if I had been bad.'

'Why?'

'The straw is rough and so I was responsible for how comfortable the baby Jesus would be when he was eventually born and put into the crib on Christmas Day.'

Billy laughed. 'A good way to get you to behave for a few weeks at least then?'

Netta nodded and laughed too, glancing at the stony face of her mother, whom, she told herself, was not laughing only because she hadn't understood what Billy had said.

'So who has been putting in the straw or the hay this year then?' Billy asked.

'Mama?' Netta asked examining the ratio of straw to hay in the crib. 'Who has been filling the crib this year?'

'Your father, me, your Opa and Oma.'

'Seems like an awful lot of straw in there this year,' Netta said her eyes flashing with mischief.

'Don't be obtuse!' Erika said with irritation although, Netta noticed, her quickly checking the crib, as if to assess if it really was full of straw.

'Well, go on then, both of you,' Martha said, coming across the room holding two steaming cups. 'Now you are here, you must add a piece too.'

Netta told Billy what her grandmother had said and they looked at each other coyly, both glancing at the pile of straw then back to each other a number of times, giggling before Billy picked up some hay and lay it in the crib. Netta allowed her hand to hover over the straw for a moment and watched as her mother's eyebrows raise in anticipation and morbid curiosity, before she snatched some hay and put it in the crib.

'Lovely, now drink!' Martha said handing over the cups.

Emilia the housekeeper came into the room from upstairs just then, welcoming Netta home and greeting Billy warmly too, before asking Erika if it was all right for her to retire for the day.

'You have a housekeeper?' Billy muttered, his eyes wide over the brim of his cup as he drank in both the tea and the relatively luxurious surroundings.

Netta attempted to laugh but saw her mother critically examining Billy's awe and she knew that disapproval had something to do with Billy's job and social status, which brought her mother's parents to her mind. 'Where are Opi and Omi?' Netta asked.

Martha and Max looked at each other despairingly as Erika said, 'They were tired. You know they like to go to bed early. You'll see them in the morning no doubt.'

Netta looked at the clock on the mantelpiece. It was

7:30 pm – too early even for the Richters to go to bed, usually. Karl came back in the room then and announced in English that Netta's things were in her old room and Billy's were in the guest bedroom across the landing, next to Emilia's room. Netta saw Billy's eyebrows twitch as the realisation that they were not permitted to share a room and certainly not a bed dawned on him. She smiled a conciliatory smile at him and he nodded back, clearly saddened but also not surprised.

'Thanks, Mr Portner. Very kind of you,' he said gallantly to Netta's grandfather and took a large gulp of tea.

13

The next day was the 23rd December and since Netta knew Christmas Eve would be a family orientated affair for everyone as ever, she seized the opportunity to meet up with her friends and show Billy off to them. A brief meeting in a coffee house had been organised followed by a matinee of a horror film starring an English actor, who spoke fluent German. Anton, a fan of the genre, had suggested that, although the film was in German, the sight of an English actor may help Billy feel more at home. Billy said he thought the idea of seeing a film first a great idea and Netta suspected, with an unhealthy dose of paranoia, that that was because he would not have to directly socialise with her friends throughout it, which disappointed her somewhat.

'Are you sure about the film?' she asked him as they entered the dining room for breakfast. 'You know you probably won't understand a single word of the dialogue.'

'It's a horror film,' Billy countered. 'How difficult can it be to follow?'

When she saw who was in there, Netta hesitated in the doorway to the dining room just enough for Billy to bump into her as he followed behind.

'Oops. You all right?' he said over her shoulder.

'Ah! The wanderer returns!' Gerhard was sitting alone at the table, finishing his breakfast.

'Hello, Opi,' Netta said, recovering herself quickly and taking a seat at the table where Emilia was laying out dishes of smoked ham, sourdough bread, quark and German sausage. 'Nobody else eaten yet?' She gestured to Billy to sit down next to her and saw him begin to form a smile with which to greet her grandfather, but since Gerhard completely ignored him his face dropped and with a furrowed brow Billy inspected the slab of jelly on his plate which had anaemic pieces of meat suspended in it.

'I'm the first,' Gerhard answered Netta. 'As usual. But then I suppose I am busier than the rest of you.'

'Well, I'm not sure Mama or Papa would agree with you since half of Mengede seem to have some kind of flu right now.'

Gerhard merely huffed. 'And how is England treating you? Like a leper, I imagine.'

'No, not at all. I'm having a wonderful time,' Netta said defiantly, wincing internally at the inaccuracy of her statement.

'Really?' Gerhard said doubtfully.

'Where's Omi?'

'Oh, she's resting. I think she has a touch of that flu you speak of.'

'Did Mama examine her?'

'Yes briefly, but she was—'

'Busy?' Netta relished the way she could argue in German with much more poise than she could in English. 'Yes, as I thought, but I'm sure they will take time out of their hectic surgeries to check on her later, as they always do.'

Gerhard seemed to have something stuck between his teeth.

Now Billy stood up, not prepared to be ignored any longer. He stuck out his hand across the table and said, 'Guten Tag. Ich bin Billy.'

Gerhard stared at Billy's hand for a moment, then wiped his own fingers on his napkin slowly before shaking the proffered hand and saying in precise English which surprised Netta almost as much as Billy, 'Welcome to our rather humble abode. I hope they are making you more comfortable than they do my wife and I.'

'Really, Opi?'

'Shush, you.' Gerhard snapped at Netta, then smiled at Billy, 'So you are English, is that so?

Netta looked anxiously at Billy but his face was bright, happy to hear his native tongue spoken by someone other than Netta; happy to be able to have a chat and not rely on her to translate.

'Well, yes I am.'

'From London?'

'No Brighton actually. It's on the south—'

'I know where Brighton is, boy. I didn't get to be such a high ranking officer in the military without a good grasp of geography. Especially of enemy territory.'

'Opi!' Netta tried to scold him, but Billy seemed unfazed.

'Well,' he parried, 'as I try to tell my father, we're not enemies any more, are we, sir.'

'But your father's generation is still in charge of your country. As is hers of ours,' he said with a disdainful nod towards Netta.

'Yeah. And if my father had his way I wouldn't even be allowed to court Netta.'

'Ah,' Gerhard darted a triumphant look at Netta, who fixed her gaze on the bread. 'He has warned you off her, has he? He might be that rare breed, a wise Englishman, after all.' He wiped his mouth and got up from his seat. 'Now, if you'll excuse me—'

But Billy wasn't finished with him. 'Well, he doesn't see *her*, really, I mean. My dad, he just sees some Nazi when he looks at Netta, not who she really is. But he'll come around, he'll have to get used to her, coz I don't plan on leaving Netta just coz of what some old codger believes, even if he is family.'

Netta's eyes widened and she looked up, at once fearful and bursting with pride at Billy's words. Gerhard pursed his lips and she wasn't sure for a moment if her grandfather was about to launch a tirade of abuse in Billy's direction.

But his eyes shone with something like amusement, even admiration, perhaps, and he nodded sharply and said, 'Well, I can't stand around idly chatting all day. Some of us have work to do. I'm off to the courthouse.'

'So remind me of their names again!' Billy said as they approached the coffee house in Dortmund, Netta leading Billy by the hand like a child to avoid the trams and the cars as they crossed the street, Billy yet to get used to which side of the road people drove on here.

'Felix is the shorter one with dark hair. Anton is fair and tall. Sophie wears glasses and Anna—'

'So this must be the boyfriend!' Anna's voice stopped Netta in her tracks as they came to the door of the coffee shop.

'Anna!'

'Don't be so surprised to see me. You invited me.'

'I know but I said noon.'

'And it *is* noon.'

'Exactly! You're never on time.'

'Well, there are some events in this world that are just too rare to miss. A total eclipse, Halley's comet. And Netta with a boyfriend – an English one at that.' She turned and dangled her hand in front of Billy as if she were an Empress who expected her ring to be kissed and said in English, 'Pleased to meet you. I am Anna.'

Billy grabbed her hand and shook it which was not a graceful motion since it was in such an unusual position to be shook. 'I'm Billy. Are you Anna, by any chance?'

He grinned.

Anna beamed.

Netta scowled.

'I like his clothes. Very elegant,' Anna said, smoke curling from her nose, as she sat with Anton and Felix on one side of the table.

Netta, who sat opposite them with Billy and Sophie, wasn't sure she liked them studying her boyfriend like an exhibit in a museum, though she agreed Billy did look fine in the same mohair suit he had worn to the seafront that day of the troubles with the rockers.

'Seems a bit tight to me. A bit feminine even,' Felix said looking down at his own loose fitting shirt and trousers as if to make sure he was still as 'masculine' as he looked in the mirror this morning.

'Oh please, Felix,' Anna sighed, 'we all know you're never going to be gracious to anyone Netta is courting.'

'Yes,' Anton chirped. 'I think he looks very smart.'

'And we all know what you're thinking with, don't we, Anton,' Felix said dropping his fist off the table into Anton's crotch.

As the two lads tussled Netta called out across the table. 'Excuse me, he is right here you know. How about talking to him rather than about him?'

'Well, does he speak German?' Felix grumbled.

'No, and you know that, otherwise you wouldn't be being so rude right in front of him,' Netta said.

'Well, then how does he expect to converse?'

'Use your English. Don't pretend you have none.'

'OK,' Felix said, sat back, took a breath and said in clear English to Billy, 'Winston Churchill: hero or warmongering villain responsible for the needless massacre of countless German civilians as well as thousands of British soldiers? Discuss.'

'Oh for God's sake!'

'Felix!'

It was Felix's turn to be punched in the crotch as everyone scolded him; everyone except Billy, and Sophie, of course, who remained quietly thoughtful. Netta was aware of Billy silently looking daggers at Felix and she stroked his thigh as you might to try and calm an agitated dog while Felix smirked, content with the furore he had created.

'What did you think of the film?' Netta asked Billy as they tumbled out of the cinema amid a crowd of excited and relieved young adults.

'I loved it,' Billy grinned, blinking at the December sun now low in the sky.

'Me too,' Anton said. 'Even better than his last film.'

'Scary as hell!' Billy went on, 'And it seemed even scarier coz it was in German, you know—' He stopped himself and Netta wasn't sure she wanted to know what he meant by that last comment, so instead she just focused on Anton who continued to recount his favourite moments from the film to Billy.

Netta had spent most of the film prising Anna's petrified fingernails out of her arm and looking just below the screen, so the horrific events unfolding above were not imprinted on her brain forever. However, now she was simply happy to see Anton and Billy grinning at each other, having shared an experience, finding common ground.

'Well, I will never get those two hours of my life back,' Felix grumbled to Anna. 'It wasn't exactly Robert Weine, was it?' he said in German, then switched to English so Billy would be sure to hear him say, 'I prefer something more intellectual, but I am sure it was perfect for Billy.'

Netta slipped her arm through Billy's and hurried him towards the car before he could react.

'All back to Netta's then?' Anton called out.

'I don't know why I bother to look this good if we end up in your dingy cellar every time we go out,' Anna sighed as she reached the car. Then she turned to Billy and said in smouldering English, 'What do *you* want, Billy?'

'Beg your pardon?' Billy seemed a little flustered.

Netta elucidated. 'She means what do you want *to do* – stay out in town or go back to mine?'

'Oh, I don't mind, whatever the majority wants to do.'

'Spoken like a true democrat,' Felix smiled insincerely and patted Billy on the shoulder.

'Yes of course I am,' Billy said, brushing off his suit jacket. 'What are you? A Nazi?'

'Billy!' Netta cried out.

Felix nodded smugly, as if he'd finally succeeded in revealing the true colours of Netta's new beau.

'Well,' Billy protested, 'He's had it in for me since the beginning.'

'Now, now, children, play nicely!' Anna said. 'Both of you in the back. I'll have to sit between you to make sure there's no misbehaving.'

'And who's going to sit between you and Billy to make sure there's no misbehaving there?' Anton said as Sophie sat on his lap in the front passenger seat.

Netta could barely concentrate on the road home as her eyes kept searching the rear-view mirror for Anna and Billy and the lack of space between them.

Anna insisted on putting some Beatles on the record player first.

'Do you know them?' she asked Billy.

'Who?'

'The Beatles.'

Billy was speechless.

Anton cackled, 'Why would he know them, you silly cow? Do you think Billy knows everyone in England?'

'Well,' Anna blushed, 'He sort of looks a bit like them, you know, his clothes and his hair, so I was sort of thinking that perhaps…' Anton was dancing around Anna copying her garbled attempt to excuse herself. 'Oh, fuck off, you!' she concluded.

'I love these beer barrel tables,' Billy said.

'Felix and I did that,' Anton said.

'Oh, nice job,' Billy said raising a glass gallantly to them both.

Felix raised his glass limply in return and muttered to Netta. 'A carpenter, really, Net. Is that the best you could do?'

'A caretaker, not a carpenter,' she snapped, wondering why she found the idea of Billy being a carpenter so offensive. 'And if you don't like it you can always leave now, Felix.'

'Sorry, sorry,' he said raising his hands in surrender. 'I'm being ungracious. I'm sure he's a lovely, *devoted* chap. If you say so.'

And they both watched as Anna continued to flirt outrageously with Billy. Netta suddenly found Anna's behaviour increasingly alarming and, after being so disappointed at the thought of Billy not wanting to socialise with her friends, she now wondered why Billy didn't move away from Anna and spend more time with her, following her around dependently as he had done since they arrived in the country.

Her brooding was broken by the sight of her father coming down the stairs wearing an apron, his hands stuffed in the front pockets.

'Don't mind me!' he said smiling at everyone. 'I'm just in the next room.' Then he said with a wink in English for Billy's benefit, 'Some surgery to attend to.'

Netta saw Billy scan her father's apron; saw him notice the spatters of blood on it as well as on his forearms. He returned Max's smile weakly and went noticeably pale.

As the party went on Netta watched Billy edge closer and closer to the door to the adjoining room, through which her father had gone. In the silences between records she saw him flinch as great bone-cracking thuds reached them through the wall. Eventually, the urge to find out just what kind of surgery this doctor was involved in was overwhelming and he shuffled through to the next room, believing he was unseen by the others, dancing and chatting as they were.

The next room in the basement was very similar to the party room in its rough, unadorned appearance, except there was a long table instead of beer barrels in front of which Max stood with his back to Billy hacking away at the raw, pink corpse lying on it. Billy gasped audibly and Max turned around. Before Billy could be seen by the killer and end up on the table himself, he slipped out of the room and straight into Netta's arms who had been watching him the whole time.

'Billy, what's wrong?' she laughed. 'You look like you've seen a ghost.'

'Oh, no, no. I didn't see anything. I just need to, erm…'

'Billy! Come on. I thought you loved all that blood and gore,' Netta said feeling strangely sadistic as she dragged Billy back into the room where her father was dismembering the corpse. 'Don't you want to watch how he does it?'

Billy looked to her as if he might either faint or begin trying to punch his way out of this house of horrors at any moment so she made sure quickly that he could see the surgery that her father was engaged in was merely the butchering of a pig in preparation for making all manner of her favourite dishes.

'Bloody hell!' Billy exhaled, partly in relief, partly in more terror at this new abomination.

Max smiled at Billy as he worked and Netta explained. 'Some of Papa's patients are farmers and they often pay for his house visits with whole pigs. We don't have a freezer, but if we make sausages and terrines and such things they will keep in sterilised conditions for a long time.' She gestured to the shelves with rows of jars waiting to be filled and Billy's face looked to Netta just like Anna's had earlier as she watched the evil protagonist on the big screen forcing bodies into enormous vats in his webbed laboratory.

'What's a terrine?' Billy asked his mouth hanging open as he watched Max work.

'It's what we had for breakfast.'

'The jelly thing?'

'Yes. It's flesh from the head of the pig pickled in the aspic.'

'Oh God.' Billy looked like he might vomit and Netta knew she shouldn't be enjoying that, but she was, and if she was honest with herself she knew it was a vindictive enjoyment which had something to do with all the time he had spent with Anna that evening.

When Billy had seen enough, which was only seconds later, they went back to the party. Anton and Anna were busy trying to do the Mashed Potato to a Chris Montez song and Felix was sifting through the records mumbling about finding something decent to play. Sophie was sitting alone at one of the beer barrel tables, her drink hardly touched, smiling sweetly at Anton or Anna whenever they called her over to dance, with clearly no intention of joining them.

'Is Sophie OK?' Netta whispered to Felix as Anna collared Billy for another dance.

''Course. Why wouldn't she be?'

'She's quiet tonight.'

'When isn't she quiet?'

'I mean, she's more quiet than usual.'

'You know Sophie, she's no doubt brewing up her latest gem to put us all in our place.' And he shouted over to her, 'Sophie! All right, Sophie?'

Netta gave Felix a discreet punch to shut him up but it was too late, all eyes were now on Sophie, who lifted up her face to them as she nodded just long enough so they could all see the sparkle from her tearful eyes.

Netta rushed over to her. 'What's wrong?'

'Nothing. Nothing, I'm fine.'

'You are not fine, my girl,' Anton said, joining them. 'Now, spit it out!'

'It's nothing really,' she said flicking her eyes towards Billy, who Anna was doing her best to keep on the dancefloor.

'Sophie?' Netta said more sternly now, concerned that her friend's tears had something to do with her boyfriend.

'I was just… just thinking about my parents. But it's OK, really.'

Anton's turn to strike Felix, but there was nothing discreet about his punch. 'Nice one, Felix, opening your big mouth again.'

'What did I say?' Felix whined.

Anton hissed quietly, 'Going on about Churchill and the war when we were in the café.'

'I didn't say anything.'

'You said enough. Clearly,' he said gesturing to Sophie as Exhibit A.

'You never speak about them,' Netta said gently.

'I hardly knew them,' Sophie said. 'I was a toddler at the time so I don't remember much. I remember the shelters. Dortmund had a labyrinth of tunnels underground. Everyone had gone down there during the air raids, but we should have left as soon as the all-clear signal was given. Everyone felt safe and secure down there, so we stayed. But when the fires took hold after the bombing they spread so fast and people got lost in the smoke-filled tunnels looking for the way out. I remember the pushing and the squeezing and the hurrying and the shoving and the tripping. I remember the screaming and then the night sky full of fireworks – or that was how it seemed to me. And I remember this knocking, frantic knocking, the kind of knocking that could only be made by a hundred people at once. It stuck in my head that sound and it was years later that I read something that finally explained it.'

'What was it?'

'There was a women's prison near the entrance to the shelter my uncle dragged me from. It was the sound of all the women locked in, banging their wooden slippers against their doors, begging to be let out as the building burned around them.'

Anton sighed, 'Bloody hell.'

'I couldn't help but imagine my parents must have made a similar sound as they tried to get out of the tunnels.'

No one knew what to say.

'Did you know,' Sophie continued, 'in one hour the British Air Force dropped twice the tonnage of bombs on Dortmund that the Luftwaffe dropped on all of England in the six months before that night. They rained down leaflets on us before the bombs. One of them had an aerial photograph of Hamburg looking like a charred skeleton of a city and the words *Time for the destruction of Germany* printed across it. The British certainly delivered on that promise. Didn't they.'

As Netta and Anton hugged Sophie, Billy came over asking if she was all right.

'She's fine. It doesn't concern you,' snapped Felix.

'No that's right, Felix,' Sophie said in a surprisingly steely tone. 'It doesn't concern him. He was a baby at the time. We were all babies at the time too. We had nothing to do with that war. And most of the population of England and Germany had nothing to do with that war, whether they fought in it or not. It wasn't like they had a choice, was it? They were just pawns. Pawns of Hitler's, pawns of Churchill's. People just trying to survive. He might be British, but he had nothing to do with the war so kindly don't use him as a pawn in your own schoolyard games, OK?'

'There's nothing bloody schoolyard about an intelligent debate on the political leaders of our—'

'Oh fuck off, Felix, will you?' Netta shouted.

And so he did.

14

It was Christmas Eve and everyone was banned from the living room while the angels and the baby Jesus went about decorating and arranging presents in there, just as they had done every year since Netta was a baby, so she decided to take Billy for a walk.

'What about Santa Claus?' Billy asked as Netta led him over the fields behind the house.

'We don't have Santa Claus. The baby Jesus delivers the presents on Christmas Eve. On the 6th of December we celebrate St Nikolaus.'

'Who's that?' Billy said breathless with the effort of negotiating the frozen clods of ploughed earth in his Chelsea boots. He had told Netta that none of his own footwear was fit for a walk in the countryside, though Netta knew he was just worried about getting his mod shoes muddy.

Netta stopped and looked over the barren fields at the grey horizon as if the past was being shown to her there like a favourite movie. 'We used to gather in the living room on the evening of the 6th and sing advent songs and read poems. Then there would be a loud knocking on the front door and we'd rush out to see a sleigh arriving in the snow drawn by horses. St Nikolaus would be on that sleigh dressed as a bishop with Knecht Ruprecht, his slave, dressed up as a chimney sweep, all black and dusty.' She heard herself giggle like a child before she went on. 'St Nikolaus would march into our living room with a golden book and a sack of presents. We would sit with big eyes in expectation of what gifts we might receive but we were also a bit frightened about how Knecht Ruprecht might punish us if we had not been good over the year. St Nikolaus would read out from his golden book all the good things we had done during the year and also remind us where we had to improve so Knecht Ruprecht would not be angry with us next year. Then he left the sack of presents and we waved him goodbye from our front door as he left on his sleigh. It was all so realistic. I wondered for many years how he knew all the things we had done over the year.'

'Who was it playing St Nikolaus and the slave?' Billy said and she saw in his eyes her own wonder.

'Years later I found out it was my Uncle Edgar and Uncle Mikel. But I could never tell at the time; they disguised themselves so well.'

'Did they do this for everyone in the street?'

'Oh no. This was just for us. My grandfather owned the horses and had the sleigh built specially by a local carpenter.' As she talked of the local carpenter she shuddered, but it could have just been the chill breeze, she told herself. And before she could brood on the sensation any longer she noticed Billy had become quiet and was looking sadly in the direction of the trees in the distance.

'What is it?' she said taking his gloved hand in hers.

'You're so lucky. Poems and songs, golden books and sacks of presents. Your massive house and your family. And all this,' he said gesturing to the bleak beauty of the landscape. 'Are you sure you want to be with someone like me?'

Netta squeezed his hand. This would be the perfect moment to tell him that she loved him; because for every moment when she wondered whether they were right for each other (and if she was honest, there were many) there were a hundred when she knew she wanted to be with him forever. She opened her mouth and saw her breath form a little fog in the space between them and she said, 'My family! They are not so wonderful. Trust me. And you live by the beach. I love the beach. It's much better than all this.'

They exchanged smiles; hers meant to warm him, his thankful for her words, but unconvinced and they walked on to the frozen lake where Netta used to skate fearlessly as a child, but now she just stood on the edge doubtful that the ice would hold her weight.

Back at the house they joined everyone in the dining room: Max and Erika, Martha and Karl, Emilia and the handful of staff from the surgery. Even Gerhard and Frieda were there and in a way Netta was more pleased to see them than the surgery staff, who, though they were invited every year, Netta still felt were somehow intruding on her family Christmas. And besides, wouldn't they rather be at home with their own families giving out presents? As this thought crossed her mind she looked at Billy smiling awkwardly at her parents' receptionist and suddenly wondered if this office worker felt as envious as Billy did about her employers' relatively opulent celebrations.

Karl played carols on the upright piano in the corner and everyone sang along, except Billy who mouthed the German words so pathetically that Netta wanted to hug him and slap him all at once. During the fourth or perhaps the fifth carol – Netta had lost count, as another glass of wine warmed her insides – she noticed her mother slip out of the room and so she wasn't surprised to hear the tinkling of bells from the living room as they finished the song.

'Oh!' Martha said with pantomime exaggeration and Netta noticed Frieda rolling her eyes, no doubt believing she could have played this role with much more aplomb. 'Listen! Could it be…? Yes! The angels have been. Come! Come!'

With childish chatter and laughter they all went through to the living room cradling their wine and as soon as Netta had confirmed the room was as beautifully decorated and as magical as ever, she kept her eyes on Billy's face hoping his reaction would be as hers had been for every Christmas she could remember. She wanted him not to be so impressed that he would doubt he fitted in here, but to be impressed enough that he would want to come back time and time again, perhaps even eventually forget his life in England and choose to remain here with her.

Billy's face shone as he took in the large pine tree decorated with burning candles casting an ethereal glow over the trestle tables covered in white linen, on which stood several piles of smartly wrapped gifts for everyone – family and staff – a card in front of each pile denoting who each one belonged to. As her father read the story of the nativity from the Bible, Billy looked at Netta with the kind of shy wonder she had hoped to see and she put her arms around him, despite imagining the raised eyebrows from Gerhard and Frieda at this public display of affection between unmarried young people. In fact it was just those withering looks which made her cling on to her boyfriend all the more in their presence, to spite them.

She knew Billy used to be the sort of boy who would mutter and moan through any religious readings or hymns in school assembly, but she also knew that it wasn't what was being read or celebrated now, but how it was being done – so meticulously, so wholeheartedly – that captured his imagination and she was bursting with pride because of it.

As he opened his gifts, Netta was constantly apologising, saying things like, 'They hadn't met you yet, so they weren't sure...' But Billy softly shooed her words away saying quite honestly, 'I would never think of getting something like this for myself, but that's why it's a great present. Thank you so much, Mr and Mrs Portner.'

'Pah!' Max replied. 'It is not us, but the angels that brought the gifts.'

'Oh yes, of course,' Billy laughed, 'Thanks, angels!' he called out to the ceiling.

Netta watched her mother as he did this and felt a stab of anxiety when she saw Erika eyeing Billy still with as much suspicion as she had on the day they had arrived.

'Would you like another beer, Billy?' Karl said.

'Ah, yes please. It's a nice beer that. What is it?'

'Dortmunder Pils. A good local drink.'

'Certainly is,' Billy said, grinning at Karl as he took his seat at the dining table.

The surgery staff and Emilia had left and just the family remained for the Christmas Eve dinner. Four couples, Netta noted and she swelled with a sense of maturity she rarely felt in this house. Her parents naturally sat at each end of the grand teak table, Frieda and Gerhard sat together on the side of the table which faced the door, as they always did. Netta and Billy had both been put strategically opposite them, so that Martha and Karl did not have to be. Of course they said it was so they were near the door so they could come and go bringing the food, but everyone knew the real reason.

'Don't worry, Mama,' Max said, 'We'll help bring things too, won't we?' He smiled at Erika.

Erika nodded.

Gerhard and Frieda did not. They were more than happy to be waited on by Martha and Karl – in fact they thought it only proper that they should be.

Netta looked at her father sitting at the end of the table with only the wall behind him, affording him a clear view of the windows and doorway. She knew, because her mother had told her, that her father couldn't sit with his back to an exit ever since he came back from the Russian labour camp; he had to be able to spot a possible threat approaching at all times. She assumed Gerhard's reason for choosing his place at the table was the same. As the wine continued to tickle her brain and prickle her face she quietly marvelled at the stories these two men could swap and the experiences that could bind them if only her grandfather wasn't so pompous as to actually refuse to acknowledge that Max's 'mere' four years in Siberia were anything like his eleven. But now Gerhard was engaged in competition not with Max, but with someone else. For despite his abrupt manner with Billy at breakfast yesterday, it seemed this evening he couldn't engage with him enough, though Netta was sure it was only to show to everyone that his English was superior to Karl's.

'A good local *brew*,' Gerhard announced.

Everyone looked at him for a little more information. Gerhard was pleased with the attention and happy to oblige.

'A brew. That is what you call a beer in England, is it not?'

'Oh, yeah. We do. Sometimes. Very good,' Billy smiled.

Netta knew the last thing that Gerhard was looking for from Billy was praise, but nevertheless she saw how he seemed to scoop it up with his eyes and whack it across the table like a ping-pong ball at Karl. 1-0.

There was a brief but awkward silence as Karl took a swig of his *brew*.

'Give me a hand bringing the main course through,' Martha said, tugging at Karl's sleeve, but he was focused on Gerhard.

'I'll help,' Max said as he jumped up trying to be helpful but only received a glare from his mother; both the glare and the reason for it went over his head, so Martha reluctantly followed him out to the kitchen.

'So, Billy,' Karl said. 'Do you have a big family?'

Netta snorted lightly into her glass – family was clearly on her Opa's mind and he no doubt felt his was too big right now. Billy was distracted by Netta's reaction and while he was looking at her Karl decided to elaborate and in doing so demonstrate his own command of the English tongue.

'I mean, do you have many, erm, cousins?'

'Oh yeah. Loads.'

Netta saw Billy register Karl's blank face.

'Erm…' Billy searched for a more proper word. 'Lots.'

Karl took a mouthful of beer.

'Many,' Billy said triumphantly.

Karl banged his glass down on the table with delight. 'Many! You have many cousins.'

'Yes. I do. My dad, my father, has two sisters and two brothers, my mum had just one brother but they all have kids, so there's a lot... many cousins.'

Netta saw Karl redden slightly as he pondered Billy's answer, then he carefully asked, 'So how many brothers do you have?'

'None.'

'And sisters?'

'One.'

'But you say you have many cousins?'

'Yeah.'

There was another awkward silence which was soon filled by the bass chug of Gerhard laughing, slow at first then increasing in speed, which reminded Netta of the evil doctor in the film they had seen yesterday.

'I think you meant siblings, Karl,' Gerhard said loudly in English.

'Mmm?' Karl sang into his glass as nonchalantly as possible.

'Siblings is the word you were looking for, not cousins,' he chortled on. 'How many siblings do you have, young man?'

'What's that, like brothers and sisters?' Billy said and Netta felt herself reddening now, both with unease at Billy's question and irritation at her grandfather for forcing him to ask it.

'Oh my God. The boy's English is as bad as yours, Karl,' Gerhard said in quick stabs of German before returning to English. 'Yes, how many brothers and sisters do you have?' he said impatiently with drops of the white wine he was guzzling on flying from his lips over the table.

'Oh. Just one. Marnie. A sister. I mean, that's her name. Marnie. She's my sister.'

'We're all hungry, I hope,' Martha said bursting into the room a lot later than she would have liked, brandishing a huge plate on which lay a whole carp.

'Wow,' Billy said as grateful for the interruption as both Karl and Netta.

'Yes, we are,' Frieda piped up. 'Who wouldn't be, at this hour?'

'Mother,' Erika warned Frieda as she followed Martha into the room with bowls of vegetables and Netta watched Gerhard and Karl eyeing each other and knocking back their drinks as if they were knocking more ping-pong balls back and forth over the fish.

'Is that a carp, Mrs Portner?' Billy asked.

'It is,' Netta cut in, drinking in a sense of pride that her boyfriend could identify the delicacy. 'How did you know?'

'I've done a fair bit of fishing in my time, you know. Used to go up Saddlescombe Lakes when I was a lad. With the old man.'

'You are a fisherman, Billy?' Karl said.

'Well...' Billy blushed.

'A man of many talents. Do you remember the caretaker of my school, Netta?' Karl said making sure that Gerhard was reminded that he was headmaster of said school. 'Herr Ritter,' Karl continued in English, his grasp of the language seemingly improving with every drop he drank – and he had by now drunk many, many drops. 'You used to play with his son Josef. A great responsibility looking after a school. One has to be an electrician, a plumber, a carpenter, everything. I merely taught. He,' he flicked a hand at Gerhard, 'merely ordered people about, but you...!'

Netta stopped listening to Karl at this point, the word carpenter setting sparks off in her mind again and she found herself looking at her mother, who in turn was staring critically at Billy. As the sparks flashed about the dark recesses of her brain they lit up the edges of memories and one in particular.

She was young. Very young. She must have been to be sitting in the basket on the front of her mother's bicycle. However, as a child she was always small for her age, so she could have been five even six then. There was man. A big tree man, that's what she had called him in her head, because he was a hulk of a man with arms like the branches of an oak tree.

Netta stroked the polished surface of the dining table as Karl and Gerhard continued to rain English on Billy in a bid to reign over each other.

That was it! The big tree man did not only look like he was made of wood he worked with wood. He was a carpenter. He had built the examination table in the first surgery her mama had just before her papa returned from Russia. She saw him haul the heavy table through the front door and into the surgery, which her Opa had made by putting up a new wall in the middle of their living room. Opa had tried to help bring in the table, but the carpenter didn't need any help. He could do it all by himself. Netta had quite admired his strength then, but at the same time she never liked the way her mother smiled at him, or the way she put her hand on those branches of his.

Back in her basket the man had met them on the street and was offering to help her mama push the bike up the hill. Netta had watched him grasp the frame of the bike in his huge knobbly fingers. She had watched her mama reluctantly let go of it and heard her say, 'My husband is back.'

Netta looked from the carpenter to her mama. They both had the same look on their faces; the look Netta herself had worn on the autumn afternoon her Opa had caught her standing on tip-toe trying to sink her teeth into one of the pears dangling tantalisingly from the tree in the middle of the garden. There was no way she could deny her crime. Her little teeth marks were there in the pear for all to see, so she got a huge telling off and had to stand under the pear tree for hours and hours in tears.

'I'll see you around.' The carpenter had said at the top of the hill as he let go of the bike, her mama almost snatching it back from him. He said it as if there was a question mark on the end.

'I think you know as well as I do it would be better if you didn't,' her mama had said and her eyes darted around the street as if the only place they were not allowed to rest was on the receding back of the big tree man.

Gerhard was mumbling to himself in German. The polar opposite of Karl where alcohol was concerned, the more he drank more unreliable his English seemed to become. Consequently Karl and Billy were chattering away in English. This delighted Netta no end as she came out of her trance, but her joy was immediately doused by her mother growling at her to help bring more food through from the kitchen.

Netta slouched after her mother like a scolded child – a somewhat inebriated scolded child – and was surprised to find her mother pressing not a bowl of carrots into her palm but a small clear plastic cup.

'What's this?' Netta said, knowing exactly what it was.

'Give me a urine sample. Tomorrow. Not now, you're full of booze.'

'Why?'

'I need to make sure.'

'Make sure of what?'

'That you're… not…' Erika stuttered as she rifled through a drawer for serving spoons. '… sick.'

'That I'm not pregnant, you mean,' Netta said slamming the cup on the counter.

'Oh for God's sake, Netta,' her mother said, wielding the found spoons like weapons as she marched back to the dining room.

Netta's head spun for a moment with possible reactions, then like a one-armed bandit in the arcade on Brighton pier, the reels of her mind eventually stopped, all three symbols the same – no lemons, melons or cherries, however, but one word: Defy. Defy. Defy. She stormed into the dining room and sat before her plate which Karl was filling with mountains of food.

'Maggots or corn?'

'What?' Netta said looking with bewilderment at her Opa then realising he was not offering her a bizarre choice of side-dishes, but talking to Billy about fishing.

'I think you can't beat a maggot,' Billy smiled.

'But they love sweetcorn. I think the bright colour attracts them to. And it's so easy to get hold of.'

'What the hell, mother?' Netta hissed in German.

Erika snapped, 'The sooner we find out the sooner we can do something about it.'

'I am not pregnant.'

'I should hope not. After all we've done for you, and you repay us with this disgrace.'

'There would be nothing disgraceful about having a child with him,' she said careful not to say Billy's name and draw his attention away from his happy debate with Karl over which method is best for reeling in carp.

'Oh please, Netta. What were you thinking? Do you think he would have taken a second look at you if you weren't from a wealthy family?'

Netta glared at the fish flesh on her plate and wanted to vomit. She could taste bile and her next words were infused with it. 'Of course, *you* would prefer it if he were a carpenter, wouldn't you!'

'Netta!' Martha squeaked, and she slapped her hand over her mouth as if she had just burped when Billy and Karl stopped chattering and looked at her. 'More fish?' she said not waiting for an answer but filling their plates and so angling them back into angling talk.

Erika took a slow deep breath and looked almost pleased that Netta had said what she had said, as if it vindicated her somehow. Netta looked up at her father who was silently watching them both with his back to the wall.

'This is what you learn over there, is it? This level of disrespect. He taught you that, no doubt.'

'Listen to yourself, mama! You're such a snob! You rail at them,' she swatted the air in Gerhard and Frieda's direction, 'for looking down on Opa and Oma and on me for that matter, but you're just the same. The apple doesn't fall far from the tree. Or should I say the pear.'

Erika looked baffled by Netta's final remark, but the idiom which preceded it hit home.

'Erika! Are you going to let her talk to you like that?' Frieda croaked.

'Once it's hooked pull it downstream. That forces it to swim against the current and it will tire out much faster,' Billy said.

'Then you've got it!' Karl cried.

'He is the only good thing about that bloody country.'

'What are you talking about?' Erika barked. 'You're doing fine there. And if you're not it's probably because he's distracting you.'

'Yes,' Gerhard said. 'I thought it was all going *wonderfully* in England. At least that's what you told us,' his sneer masquerading as a smile.

'Well it's not,' Netta said, her desire to upset her mother with this news far more powerful now than her need to pretend her life in England was all roses. 'It's shit actually. And it's all your fault,' she said with her arms wide open indicating them all, except Billy of course.

'Well, how on earth did you come to that warped conclusion, missy?' Gerhard chuckled.

Netta could barely contain her frustration. 'Why didn't you stop them?'

'Who?'

'You all think you're so high and mighty. Military officers, doctors, teachers. All of you were in positions of authority then. You had a platform from which to speak out, make a stand. If you had, perhaps the atrocities would never have happened.'

'What do you mean?'

'The Nazis, Mama. The Jews.'

Erika paled and took an unusually large draught on her wine.

'We didn't know what was happening to the Jews back then.' Although Netta's father spoke in a low sombre voice, because he had not spoken for so long now, his voice cut through the row and hooked Netta's ear. 'The first I knew of it was when I was in a cattle truck on the Siberian railway, on my way to the labour camp. The train ground to a halt, as it did often, for hours sometimes and then I would peek out from between the slats to try and fathom where we were, but everything always looked the same: flat and snow covered. I think we were passing through Poland when I saw the bodies. Rows and rows of them. I couldn't work out what I was seeing at first. It looked like furrows of ploughed earth between the swathes of snow. And then I saw their striped prison shirts and the gold Star of David sewn on each.'

Netta wanted him to go on. There was so much she didn't know about him, so much he hadn't said. But she was sad to see that he seemed to shrink back to the wall then and almost become a part of it.

'Our butcher was a Jew. So was the baker,' Martha said. 'Then one day they and their families were gone. When we asked about them we were told they had been relocated. There wasn't enough room for them all. They said.'

'And you believed that? You accepted that?'

'Eat your food,' Martha urged Netta limply.

But she would not be silenced. 'There were thousands

139

of camps all over this country. How could you not know?'

'We couldn't be sure,' Erika said curtly and Netta was glad her mother had spoken again – she was finding it hard to be angry at her Oma and her father.

'How *sure* do you need to be before you do something? Before you stand up against genocide?'

'We were afraid of what they might do to us too.'

'You were unconscionable cowards.'

'How dare you!' Gerhard slammed his fork on to his plate.

'I'm not sick with child, Mama, I'm sick with worry because I'm harassed every day in England just because I'm a German. And would you stand up and speak out against someone who persecuted me just because of my race or my religion?'

Erika was exasperated. 'Of course.'

'Then why not them?' Netta shrieked and she looked around to see Billy and Karl, their mouths wide open, like two caught fish.

15

erhard and Frieda did not come to Midnight Mass, not because they were incensed with Netta's behaviour, though they were, but simply because they were Protestants. Erika, Max, Martha and Karl also seemed to Netta to be incensed with her outburst at dinner, but that didn't keep them from going to the church, in fact it seemed to propel them to go sooner – the more time they all had in the purifying house of God the better!

On the way to mass Netta huddled against Billy as they walked several paces behind the others. He asked in hushed tones what all the fuss at dinner was about.

'Oh, nothing,' she said.

'Didn't sound like nothing.'

'Family politics that's all. I told you they were a pain.' They walked on in silence for a while with nothing to be heard but the murmur of her family's anxious conversation up ahead (no doubt about her, she thought) and the soft crunch of snow underfoot. 'You seem to be getting on with my grandfather really well.'

'Which one?' Billy said mischievously.

'This one,' she said pointing to her Opa ahead. 'Obviously.'

'Yeah. He's groovy. I like him.'

'Me too,' Netta said.

She looked forward to mass now knowing that Billy would see her Opa conducting the choir and playing the organ, and she felt an extra buzz of pride when she sat next to Karl at the organ and operated the bellows for him, knowing Billy's smiling eyes would be on them both.

When they got home it was nearly 1 am. Everyone hurried to their beds exhausted, especially when they saw

Gerhard sitting in the living room alone sipping port. But Netta felt Billy holding back, saw him looking almost pitifully at her Opi.

'Gooten Nighcht, Herr Richter,' he said in his awful attempt at German. 'Und froilicking Weinachting.'

'Oh dear me,' Gerhard snorted at Netta. 'I thought you were a German teacher. Haven't taught this one very well, have you?'

'You never give up, do you, Opi,' Netta grumbled.

'No, I don't. Nor do you for that matter.'

As he spoke those words, Netta saw herself in England, a meek young woman, unsure of herself, envious of Rita as she took no nonsense from Billy's father.

'We're sure the British education system won't know what has hit it when you get stuck into it,' Anna had said at her farewell party. But Netta felt more hit than hitter when it came to the British education system so far.

'If you had served over a decade in prison for telling the truth when others had escaped by lying, I don't think you of all people, Netta, would let that go without a fight,' Sophie had said at the same party. They all thought of Netta as a fighter, one who wouldn't let things drop. And now even her Opi, it seemed, thought the same of her. She felt disappointed with, almost ashamed of, her 'English' self.

'And I have a feeling neither does he.' Gerhard held up the bottle of port to Billy and said in English. 'Care for a glass?'

'It's very late,' Netta said as she saw Billy's eyes flash.

'What is that?' he said. 'Port? Very posh. Don't mind if I do,' and he sat on the sofa while Gerhard poured him a glass. 'Nets?'

Netta remained standing, keen to go to bed and get away from Gerhard, but more determined not to leave Billy alone with him. So she sat. Gerhard poured a third glass, but she noticed he didn't take another sip from his all night – perhaps, she thought, since he was speaking with Billy, he wanted to maintain a decent level of English, if only to piss on Karl's valiant attempt earlier. But he addressed her first.

'So the English are proving a little... prejudice, are they? Present company excepted, of course.'

'Yes,' Netta sighed. 'Not all of them, but... yes. And although the bigots infuriate me, I can't help but sympathise, with some of them anyway.'

'What about you, young man? Is everyone in your family happy with you courting a German?'

Billy looked at Netta as if asking her permission to reveal the truth. Netta shrugged ever so slightly so Billy went on, 'My dad isn't, as I said before, but he fought in the war. He's got scars, you know, and not just physical ones, I s'pose.'

'Hmm,' Gerhard thought for a moment, then added. 'And yet when all your community is telling you to stay away from this little "Nazi", here you are.' He raised his glass to salute Billy and Netta felt her feelings towards her grandfather thawing a little – but that could have been just the port, she told herself.

Nevertheless, she found herself saying, 'How's the court case going?'

Gerhard winced. 'I think it will be the death of me frankly. Funny, ey? I survived hell in the freezing labour camps of Siberia, but a warm comfortable court room will be the thing that finishes me off.'

'How long did you spend in the camps, sir, if you don't mind me asking, like?' Billy asked.

'Eleven long years.'

'Wow.'

'Indeed,' Gerhard said, and Netta tried to fight the sense she had that he enjoyed telling people how long he had been imprisoned, as if it was a badge of honour. 'It was 1945 when we were captured. May 8th. We were surrounded by the Russians. The only way out was by sea. We waited and we waited, but no boats came. Then I was sent the command to effect an honorary capitulation. Honorary capitulation! That's a contradiction in terms if ever I heard one, ey? I was told we would probably be interned, but that officers would get to keep their weapons. From time to time, I went down to the shore. There were thousands and thousands of people, wandering around aimlessly, hoping there would still be another boat. I sincerely hoped there would not be.'

'Why?' Netta asked.

'Because there would be far too many people trying to get on board so close to the ceasefire. It would be chaos. But then midnight, came and everyone seemed to have quietened down, with most of them lying on the ground, just waiting. No one was complaining, we were all deep in thought, remembering loved ones back home. You know, it was truly unbelievable what lay behind us and unfathomable what was about to come. I had no idea what would happen. All I knew was that my daughter was safe and expecting her first child...'

Netta was moved by the notion of her Opi thinking about her even before she was born.

'... And that her husband was a doctor, and that my wife had said she would not leave our factory and all our employees until she was carried out kicking and screaming.'

'Were you responsible for all those men?' Billy asked.

'My regiment numbered two thousand, five hundred. I reported to the Russians that there were two thousand, two hundred, because some of the men were badly wounded and dying and I didn't want the Russians to make up the numbers in their usual manner, by forcibly taking healthy local people.'

'Would they really do that?' Billy asked, incredulous.

Gerhard nodded. 'And as we were marched out a

Russian officer stands in front of me and demands my pistol. I say, "No, I am an officer and that is not part of the capitulation agreement." He shouts "No, you are not!" and he places the barrel of his pistol between my eyes.'

'Blimey!'

'Indeed! I have no choice, do I not? I hand over my gun. I need to stay alive to lead my men.'

Netta looked at Billy, who was now perched on the edge of the sofa, and even she was anxious to hear more from her grandfather.

'At night, we would sleep in the fields and a few of the Russians would come and try to beat us and take everyone's watches. I tried repeatedly to communicate with my Russian counterpart, to sort out these drunken thieves, but he would simply say, "That's just how it is."'

'Where did they take you?'

'Minsk.'

'That must have been tough.'

'Tough would be putting it mildly. It was a frozen hell. They fed us only some watery grey-green soup made from the leaves of a tree, with the stalks still in it. Sometimes, there would be husk in it, making it taste very bitter, and sometimes there would be a few fish bones. We were given two hundred grams of very hard bread. It was so disgusting I often chose not to eat anything. I would rather go without, no matter how painfully hungry I was, than insult my body by eating that rubbish.'

A shadow of a smile passed briefly over Netta's lips – that was her stubborn old Opi all right!

'As the time passed slowly, many of my men didn't see the sense in going on.'

'I bet,' Billy said. 'I wouldn't have lasted five minutes.'

'But you must!' Gerhard hissed at Billy and Netta suddenly felt she was a fly on the wall of those mouldy, windswept barracks, watching her grandfather talking to a fellow officer, not Billy, as they sat shivering on their bunks. 'You must save your dignity. It is more important now than ever before to hold on to it, I told them. You must be able to strive forward, but you must also be an example. If you have to go hungry and keep on being hungry, do so with self-respect, even if you are sure you are going to die. Do not take the faith of the younger captives away from them: they had trusted in Germany and in their elders, and had gone into battle, even though most of them were to lose their lives. Show them they can still have self-respect, because, once the belief of the young is destroyed, you will never be able to bring it back.'

Netta's stomach churned at these words. Images of her young students in England scudded across her mind and she was filled with a yearning to hurry back to the classroom.

'We should only see our small personal fate in relation to the whole of what is happening around us,' Gerhard went on, 'then we will recognise the deep sense of our misery and why it was necessary, why it could not be avoided. If you say, "Why me?" I say, "Why not you?" Be proud that you are part of those chosen to be an example, show that you want to be a part of this. There will be others who cannot take it, but that does not matter – you need to be an example to the weak ones, to the second and third ranks who will moan and complain. They are also the... tools of fate. Be grateful that, because of your strength and your heart, you don't belong to *them*.' Netta guessed that he meant the Russians, because he spoke as if he was no longer in the warm living room, but back in the camp again. 'If you never dare to rattle the cage then you will never find the strength to survive.'

Netta was grateful that the table lamp beside Gerhard was the only light on in the whole shadowy room and wiped at her eyes before he saw the tears.

'Every night they would drag us out one by one for interrogation. The first one to try his luck with me thought he was a martial arts hero, but actually he was an oily flannel. "Who are your friends?" he whined. "My friends are all dead," I said. "With whom do you socialise then?" "I socialise with no one." "Well, you must talk to somebody sometimes. Who are in the bunks next to yours?" I told him and he asked me what we spoke about. I told him, "We speak about the state of our bowels and the lack of food." He was angry at my answers, but I was merely telling the truth. Cake?' He suddenly came out of his trance and held out a plate of cakes oozing with fresh cream, left over from dinner.

'No thanks,' Billy said in an almost-whisper.

It felt almost wrong, after what Gerhard had just told them, to indulge, but Netta could never resist her grandmother's hazelnut torte.

Gerhard laughed, 'Martha knows how to make a cake, I'll give her that, at least!' And through mouthfuls of gateau he carried on with the story of his interrogation, Netta imagining that the way the cake sometimes muffled his words was the way his words really would have been distorted by the swollen lips and broken teeth he received during those barbaric interviews.

"'Are you a member of the National Socialist Party?" said the oily flannel. "I am," I said. "Why?" he demanded. "Because of my convictions," I said. "And what are they?" Well this made me impatient and I said, "Are you not a socialist? Then you should know." The oily flannel didn't like that and after he'd dealt me a few punches I decided it was best to elaborate. "In my homeland," I told him, "there were enormous numbers of unemployed people – seven million registered – families with children in great misery. We had the mines and the textile industry, but nothing worked. For fourteen years, the ruling parties were unsuccessful in helping these people. Then Hitler came along and it cannot be denied that his party brought about total employment, good roads, everyone had food and no one had to live a miserable existence any longer." "Those roads were built in preparation for an attack on the Soviet Union," the fool insisted. "Poppycock!" I said, "If he had built the motorways to have a war against the Soviet Union, he would have built them from west to east, from Berlin to Silesia, to Western Prussia and so on, but they went south to Bavaria and north to Hamburg, nothing towards the east. If you doubt me, look at a map!"'

Gerhard thumped the arm of the chair in which he sat and, as a puff of dust motes exploded from it, caught in the lamp light, Netta saw Billy jump as if that little explosion was caused by artillery fire.

'My interrogator asked me my views on German foreign policy. I told him I thought it was terrible. Well, if it had been any good we would not have lost the war and I wouldn't have been stuck in that hell hole, would I? He asked me whether I agreed with Hitler's conviction that Germany was a nation without space. I told him it was. "Check the statistics," I said. "Compare it to France, for example, square kilometre to square kilometre. He then implied I was one of those officers who had my sights set on a big mansion by a Russian river. What an arse! "I have my own mansion already," I told him, "Why would I want to go to Russia to have…?"'

Netta watched as Gerhard swallowed the rest of the sentence. He reached out instinctively for the port, but let his hand fall lightly onto the table instead and his fingers just tapped the surface for a moment. For all the ungrateful words he had not swallowed about living here in this house, all the grumblings and criticisms of Martha, Max and Karl even though he had nowhere else to go, Netta felt unusually sorry for Gerhard right then when, in material terms at least, she could see just how much he had lost since the war.

Billy had no such aversion to taking more port. 'You're a braver man than I,' he said between sips. 'Standing up to those Russians like that. I might have crumbled under all that interrogation.'

'Don't sell yourself so short, boy.' Gerhard said. He didn't give Billy a chance to respond as he was clearly keen to explain to him, 'I didn't need to crumble, as you put it. Those who are lying crumble. Eventually. I hope.'

'And you were telling the truth,' Netta said quietly, almost to herself.

'Of course. And I knew I might be signing my own death warrant by doing so, but I asked myself all along what would it be like for the young soldiers seeing me lie my way out of this situation, as most of my fellow officers were doing. I would be a coward. I had a responsibility to my son. How could I face him again if I lied? I hoped that I had brought him up to be true to himself and have the strength of his own convictions.'

Gerhard snorted lightly as if at some tasteless joke. Netta couldn't help but wonder where his daughter, Erika, featured in his deliberations about responsibility and the thought tussled with her admiration for his honesty until he went on, those tapping fingers of his now fiddling shakily with the lapel of his jacket.

'Occasionally postcards from home got through, unless the Russians decided to throw them away. Sometimes I wish they'd thrown away the one your grandmother sent. But I have a feeling they couldn't wait to see the look on my face when I read it.'

'Why?'

'It said that Dieter, my son, had been killed in action. He was only twenty. Just a boy.'

Netta watched his fingers grip the lapel tightly now, as if to steady his whole being. And, though she knew her mother's brother had died before Netta was born, Netta had never considered the circumstances and their impact on her grandfather, since she had spent most of her young life being, at the very least, irritated with him.

'That's terrible,' Billy offered.

'I'll tell you what was terrible,' Gerhard growled. 'Terrible was writing back to my wife. Telling her: *Keep thinking about the happy times we all had together. Hold on to that*, and not knowing if the letter would ever reach her. Not that it would have mattered if the bastards had ripped up my letter before it even left the camp, because Frieda was taken away to a Polish prison shortly after Dieter died so she never received the letter anyway.' He let out a parched, wry laugh. 'Do you know what, Billy?'

Netta was pleasantly surprised to hear Gerhard call Billy by his name for the first time.

'What, sir?'

'The only lie I ever told during my time in that camp was in that letter. To my wife.' He looked at Billy through eyes that sparkled with tears. Netta saw Billy shift in his seat awkwardly.

'Oh?' Billy said.

'Yes. I wrote, *Everything is OK here. No need to worry about me.*'

Billy stuttered as he tried to find the right thing to say, but Gerhard saved him the trouble as he had returned to his trancelike state and was staring at the mantelpiece as if it were the barren miles beyond the barbed wire fence of that camp.

'I had been running one morning. I had decided, you see, that getting fit, and getting rest and sleep were the most important things now. Every morning I would run a circuit of the prison yard. And every morning as I ran past I would see the sacks of potatoes which had been left to rot behind the kitchens. Food that could have been nourishing my men. Anyway, as I caught my breath looking out through the fence I saw a truck driving down the road. That was a very rare event I can tell you. And I just knew they were coming for me. Two officers jumped down from the truck. I remember the senior one looking very, very smart indeed. His blond hair was neatly parted in the centre, his skin was immaculate. I remember because I couldn't believe someone so well presented could seem so ugly. But he dripped with unpleasantness. He marched up to me brandishing a knife – you know one that you can fold in two.'

'A flick knife,' Billy said with a blend of excitement and horror.

'Yes that's it. Well, he marched up to me and without a word stuck this knife into my trousers and cut them off me so I stood there in the cold in just my underwear.'

'Bastard.'

'Indeed. The junior one thought this was great sport, he was grinning like a loony as he set fire to my clothes on the ground and threw the wallet he'd found in my trousers onto it. That wallet had been a gift from Dieter, you know. All that it had left in it were photos.'

Netta watched her Opi's enormous Adam's apple rise and fall as he swallowed drily.

'Of the family.' He paused.

Netta put her hand on the small of Billy's back and she knew from the way his chest rose and fell that it was a welcome sensation for him.

'I'm sorry,' Gerhard said, perhaps noticing Netta's action and misreading its intention. 'You must want to go to bed.'

'No,' Netta said. 'Go on, Opi. If it's OK with you.'

Gerhard looked at her with something like gratitude in his eyes, but it was hard for Netta to tell, both because of the low light and the fact that he'd never looked at her or anyone else in this house with gratitude before.

'They drove me to another compound where the staff quarters were. I was led down a long, dark corridor and told to sit and wait. It was eleven o'clock in the morning by then. I had a feeling they would keep me waiting for hours, so I lay down on the floor and slept.'

Gerhard noticed Billy's surprised expression.

'You learn to sleep anywhere anytime in those conditions. And I knew I had to preserve my energy.' He smiled, 'And, just as I thought, they woke me more than twelve hours later with a firm boot in my rib cage. I was dragged to a dimly lit room and made to stand in front of a desk behind which sat that same senior officer; he was a colonel I realised as I examined his uniform more closely. His secretary and translator sat next to him. She was very tall, very thin – she reminded me of a spear – and spoke excellent German. Through her translations, the colonel told me he needed to gather sufficient information before condemning an officer and that I had been observed – spied upon it seems – for some time already. He read from a file full of papers that, "On September 4th at 3 am you said to the staff officer, *Don't think that they will let us go home any time soon. Don't forget we are in the hands of the cruellest enemy who will do with us whatever they wish.* Did you say that?" he asked me. Well, some of my men had got it into their heads that we would be home in time for Christmas. I knew this was nonsense so I had to try and stop them getting their hopes up, otherwise the disappointment would kill them. So I told the colonel that it was true, I did say that. Then he asked me if I'd told the men not to work harder than necessary as it wouldn't get them home any quicker. I told him this was true too – after all I had to help the men preserve their energy, especially since they were so deprived of decent food. And he asked if I knew a man called Stachel. I told him I'd never heard of the man, though he insisted I did, but I replied that there were five hundred men crammed in one room in our barracks; it wasn't possible for me to know all of them by name. So he kept on at me, asking me what I did when I was abroad in Italy, Switzerland, Greece – I was surprised he knew I'd been, actually – and was I a spy? And am I a friend or an enemy of the Soviet Union? "I have nothing against the Russian people," I said, which made the colonel impatient, and he demanded, "I don't want to know how you feel about the Russian people, I want to know how you feel about the Soviet Union!" I knew what it meant if I answered his question directly, so I kept trying to stall, insisting "I have already told you, I have nothing against the Russian people. There are good and bad in every nationality." The officer's temper was rising now and he bellowed at me, "But the Soviet Union! The Soviet Union!"'

And Gerhard beat his fist on the arm of his chair again, just as the colonel had no doubt beaten his desk.

'So I said, "If you mean the system, I have to say that I completely reject it. What you do on your side of the fence is of no interest to me, as long as you let us do what we feel is right for us on our side of the fence." It was then that I almost missed the oily flannel, since this colonel had a much better left hand on him. He leapt across the desk like a wild animal and punched me to the floor, shouting, "Many words! Many words! I just want a yes or a no. Are you a friend or an enemy of the Soviet Union?" "Well, if you really want to know that," I said, "then I have to say that I am an enemy of the Soviet Union."'

'Bloody hell!' Billy cried out, and Netta wasn't sure if it was because of Gerhard's predicament or the fact that she had just sunk her nails into his back, engrossed as she was in her Opi's story. 'What did they do to you when you said that?'

'They tortured me and sentenced me to twenty-five years solitary confinement and hard labour.'

'Jesus. Why didn't you just tell them what they wanted to hear?'

'Why don't you just court a nice English girl so no one will bother you?'

Billy and Gerhard exchanged a long wide-eyed look at the end of which Billy smiled, nodded and drained his glass of port.

'They showed me a letter once as they tortured me.'

Netta was burning to know exactly how they tortured him, but she felt it would be perverse to ask and she knew that if he ever did give her the details of those sessions, she would wish she had never known; wish she could take a scouring pad and scrub the images from her mind as easily as Emilia would scrub the pots and pans clean tomorrow night when she returned to work. But Netta knew that would be impossible. So she kept quiet.

'It was a letter from this Stachel man, whom the Colonel had claimed I knew. He had written to the colonel a grovelling letter about how he knew me well and that I was his commander; that he did and said everything I ordered him to; and that when the colonel saw how sorry he was, he hoped, begged that his sentence would be reduced. The swine! I had never met the man. He, like so many others, lied through his teeth to get out after a couple of years and, like so many other officers, mistreated his own men just to get in the good books of the Russians. So they were soon released and I… well, I wasn't. I would listen to the radio; the only people who were prisoners in the USSR, it said, were those who had committed crimes against humanity. I of course couldn't let this lie and so I wrote to Stalin himself.'

'Did you?' Netta said with a degree of admiration in her tone.

'Why not? No one is above reproach, my girl, if they have done wrong. Remember that! I brought to his notice that (1) I had never been accused of any crime against humanity nor had any judgement been made against me; and (2) I was supposed to be a spy. Well, even if I were sentenced to prison for espionage, according to the Russians I should not be in their territory any longer. So I asked for immediate reparation.'

'And is that when they released you?'

'God, no. He completely ignored my demands. That was 1953. I was stuck there for another three years. Until

1956 when Chancellor Adenauer, and Khrushchev finally struck a deal over POWs. That is when I finally came home… Well, came here anyway,' he said gesturing dismissively to the bricks and mortar around him, which sobered Netta up somewhat and made her long for her bed again. 'Our factory, our entire business had been taken from us of course, as had the villa. But I finally did meet Stachel, you know. And all the rest of the little shits that lied their way out of prison. All of them now doing very nicely thank you very much, in government positions, so perhaps you can see why I will not rest until—'

'Opi?' Netta sat forward. 'Opi?' She stood up and went to crouch in front of her grandfather who was clutching his head and trying to speak, but nothing was coming from his mouth except soft moans and then a trail of drool. He was leaning so much to one side that Netta had to stop him from falling out of the chair. 'Billy, get my parents!'

'Opi, Opi,' she cooed, 'come on, Opi, you need to tell me more of your story. I want to hear more. You're not done yet.'

Even Netta, to whom every second now seemed like an hour, was surprised at how quickly Billy returned with her parents. They fell into the room almost brawling as they competed to be the doctor who would first diagnose the problem.

'Papa!' Erika screeched as she rushed in.

'Erika, step back! You can't see things clearly,' Max shouted as far as this softly spoken man could ever shout.

Netta held onto her mother, knowing that her papa wasn't just referring to the tears welling in Erika's eyes.

'His heart?' Erika said.

'Was he worked up?' Max asked Netta. 'Angry?'

'No. Well, he was just telling us about his time in Siberia and—'

'Oh, Netta,' Max growled, 'It doesn't help to drag all that stuff up.'

But Netta knew her father wasn't talking about her Opi
– well, not only her Opi.

'Did he grab his arm before this happened?' Erika said
grabbing Netta's arm as if to demonstrate, though Netta
couldn't help feeling her mother was holding on unneces-
sarily hard to punish her for some reason.

'No, no, definitely not.'

'Did he say he had a headache? Did he hold his head or
slur his speech?' Erika said.

'Erm… Erm…' Netta couldn't think clearly amid the
barrage of angry questions.

'Think!'

Netta imagined the last few minutes like a reel of film
being pulled backwards through a projector, and then she
saw it. 'Yes, yes. He held his head just before.'

'Max, it's a stroke.'

'Yes. Get some aspirin!' Max said, though Erika was
already out of the room heading to the surgery to get
some.

Netta watched with a morbid fascination as her father
loosened her Opi's collar and, with Billy's help, laid him on
the sofa as if he was putting a baby down. She had never
seen her cantankerous grandfather looking so vulnerable
and subdued.

'Call the hospital!' Erika barked at Max as she returned
with the drugs and shoved him aside. And, as much
as she felt abused by her mother's roughness in those
moments, Netta also watched her with envy-clad awe as
Erika, having confidently made her diagnosis, began the
necessary treatment with conviction.

16

Netta was more upset by her grandfather's illness than she ever thought she would be, but she had to admit to herself that she was also miffed that the festive Christmas Day she had hoped to show off to Billy was now, not surprisingly, a more muted affair than usual. However, since tradition and Erika's parents' usual unwillingness to participate dictated that they kept themselves holed up in their room, the fact that they were both now in holed up in Dortmund hospital almost seemed like a minor detail. Erika too stayed with them and, although the house was busy with the customary descent of Netta's aunts and great aunts from her father's side of the family bringing boxes and boxes of homemade cream cakes, it was her mother's absence that made the shift in mood undeniable to Netta, no matter how much beer and Black Forest gateau she consumed.

'Come on!' she said to Billy, pulling him by the hand away from one of the aunts who was trying to explain, mainly by means of mime, the best way to cook the dumplings he had enjoyed so much at lunch.

'Where are we going?' he said with an apologetic smile at the aunt.

'I need to get out of the house. Let's go for a walk.'

'Oh no, not over the fields again,' Billy said, looking mournfully down at his Chelsea boots.

'No, no, we'll stick to the paths and roads this time. Come on!' Netta pleaded. 'There's so much more to show you.'

'More of what?' Billy said a little impatiently as he went to find his parka.

Netta mused on this as she waited for him. More of what? What *did* she mean, there's so much more to show

him? More of the country? More of Mengede? Well... More
of her childhood – that's what she meant. She wanted to
take him on a tour of the places that were landmarks in
her youth. It was important to her that he knew as much
about her past as possible. Partly she knew this was
in order to try and eliminate the image she believed he
had of her as a rather reserved, even submissive woman
fumbling through her life in England, though a voice in
her chattering brain suggested that it was that reserved,
even submissive woman fumbling through her life in
England that he fell in love with in the first place, so would
it be wise to show him she was anything else if she wanted
to keep hold of him? She promptly told the voice to shut
up, since the other thing driving her to take him on a tour
of her past was the fact that already she couldn't conceive
that he wouldn't be present for any part of her future. This
notion both thrilled and terrified her, and though it was
difficult to distinguish the effect of the two emotions on
her body, right then she was sure she was thrilled to be
trussed up with Billy in this way.

She showed him the canal first with its banks sloping
sharply from the fields, down which she used to race her
friends, always beating the boys, she was keen to point
out, even if it did result in her crashing into the water
sometimes. Then the primary school where Karl was the
headmaster and where they used to go to wash because
many years ago the school showers were so much warmer
and stronger than theirs at home. Then the secondary
school where the nuns educated her by pulling her hair
and whacking her head until the day her father's motorbike
roared into the car park and he proceeded to humiliate
Sister Hildegarda by out-quoting her when it came to verses
of the Bible, which she so desperately tried to use to justify
her treatment of the children. It was only years later, Netta
told Billy, that she realised her father had suffered so much
corporal punishment in the labour camps of Siberia he was

not prepared to let anything like it happen in peacetime to his daughter – unless he meted it out himself, of course.

'Did he? Did he hit you?' asked Billy, bristling protectively.

'Of course he smacked me, when I was naughty,' she replied. 'Didn't yours?'

'Oh… yeah, 'course.'

'And next door over here,' Netta said like a ringmaster, 'is the bakers. All the other kids would give me their money and dare me to bunk over the wall during break time. Then I'd run here to buy them all doughnuts. And they would put in extra pfennigs so that I would get mine for free for completing the dare.'

The shop was closed now, but Billy and Netta stood at the window and admired the pastries that remained.

'My God! Doughnuts, Black Forest gateau, hazelnut cream cake, what is it with you Germans and fat?' he said, echoing Netta's own criticism of his father's love of dripping, and she grinned and playfully punched him.

'Touché,' she said.

'Ah, the prodigal daughter returns.'

The voice sent shivers down Netta's spine. It was a cold turkey-gobble of a voice and unmistakably Sister Hildegarda's. Netta turned. Apart from the few grey hairs poking out from the side of her wimple, Netta was surprised to see that the nun didn't seem to have aged at all, but that was probably, she told herself, because her face had always been wrinkled with disdain.

'Sister,' Netta said curtly, not even bothering to introduce her to Billy, nor to speak in English for his benefit.

'I hear you've been in England,' Hildegarda said with more than a dollop of disbelief. 'What on earth were you doing there?'

'Teaching,' Netta said, blushing since she was both embarrassed to share the profession of this nun and yet reddening with a desperation to point out somehow how her brand of teaching was nothing like this dinosaur's.

'Teaching?' Hildegarda emitted a schoolgirl snort. 'You? Teaching what?'

'German.'

'To the English?'

'Well, who else do you think populates England?' Netta sniped.

'Well, it seems unqualified German girls do now,' Hildegarda countered and then she began speaking in English as if to prove her point. 'And how do you speak English now?'

'Through my mouth,' Netta wanted to say in order to illuminate the nun's imperfect effort, but she held her tongue – for now.

'If you are teaching English children I hope your English is perfect.'

Netta noticed Billy's attention was piqued now he could understand the women's words and she addressed the nun by her name to let him know exactly who this relic on the historical tour of her childhood was.

'Well, yes, actually, Sister Hildegarda, I think it is pretty good.'

'Pretty? What are you saying, girl? I think you mean very. Good Lord, I am sorry for the English children.'

'No, no, I meant *pretty* good. But I am being modest. My English is excellent actually, no thanks to you.'

The nun ruffled her habit and her folded face reddened as she gobbled at the air searching for a response.

'Oh yes,' Netta laughed, 'I see it now! My father always said you looked like an overgrown turkey whenever he confronted you about your dire methods.'

It was Billy's turn to snort like a schoolkid.

'I beg your pardon?' Hildegarda gobbled.

'I'm sorry, I can say it in German if it would be easier for you.'

Hildegarda was speechless.

'Now, if you'll excuse us we're going to the *butcher* for some pork.'

She heard Billy inhale ready to speak, ready to tell her that surely the butcher, just like the baker, was closed on Christmas Day and besides, her father had a basement heaving with jars of pickled pork, so why on earth would they need to go to the butcher now? So she gently nudged him back into silence while Hildegarda, just as Netta knew she would, took the bait.

'Ah, you mock, girl, but you are not correct even with the simplest of words.'

'What do you mean?' Netta said disingenuously.

The nun inflated herself with a sense of imminent victory. 'It is butt-cher, girl. *Butt*-cher. I say, as always, nothing will become of you, Portner. Hallelujah! Amen.'

'Erm, excuse me,' Billy said. 'But no, it's not.'

Hildegarda was not surprised that the Portner reprobate had a fancy man hanging off her, but she was shocked to hear him speaking English too and she shook her red flapping jowls in his direction now.

'It's not butt-cher,' said Billy. 'The word is most definitely *butcher*. Trust me.'

'And what do you know about the English language, young man?'

'I'm English. I'm from England. That's what, love.'

Netta giggled uncontrollably and, taking Billy's hand, she almost skipped away leaving the overgrown turkey gobbling longingly at the sinful pastries locked behind the baker's window.

17

'Apparently I am *allowed* to go home today,' Gerhard said with all the sarcasm of someone who was acutely aware of his freedom to go wherever he wanted whenever he wanted. Netta could appreciate his indignation, knowing now how long and how severely he had been deprived of his liberty before. But she could also hear the way his speech was slightly slurred and she wondered if he was recovered enough to go.

'Well, that's good,' Netta said. 'But are you sure you're ready?'

'The doctors here would have kept me in longer, but since I live with a Dr Portner and a Dr Portner they are happy to *release* me into their care.'

Netta smiled at the image he had unwittingly conjured for her of such a safe and secure home and it made it all the harder for her to think about leaving.

'I have to go.'

'Well, that's fine, go on, I don't need babysitting,' Gerhard said defensively.

'No, not now, Opi. I meant I have to go back to England tomorrow.'

'So soon? But the Christmas holidays aren't over yet?' her grandfather said trying to sound irritated by Netta's bad time management, but betraying a sense of loss beneath it.

'Well the English school holidays end sooner than ours here.'

'Before Epiphany?'

Netta nodded.

'Well, that's typically heathen of them.'

Netta laughed briefly then looked up and down the ward at all the other sick and injured attached to their drips, dripping with the rhythm of unwound clocks, and she felt as if she'd just been injected with a large dose of urgency.

Gerhard continued, 'So you won't be here to have your mother's sponge cake on the 6th. You won't be in with a chance of getting the slice with the coffee bean in it.'

'No.'

'Thank God for that. Could never bear it when you got to be king for the day. Bossing everyone around.'

'And how was that different from any other day?' Netta grinned.

'Oh it wasn't, except we all had to bite our tongues because tradition said you had carte blanche to do so.'

'Well, not this year Opi. But I'm sure that'll be fine with you. Gives you a better chance of getting it. And God help the family if you do.'

'Oh, no, no I shan't be partaking in such childish games. I've got work to do.'

'Really?'

'Of course. Don't you listen? I'm in the middle of court proceedings, girl.'

'Well, I believe the doctors' orders were complete bed rest.'

'Who told you that?'

'Dr Portner and Dr Portner.'

'Poppycock!'

'Opi, you can't be over-exerting yourself.'

'I won't be. I'll be sitting in a courtroom.'

'Your life is at stake.'

'There is so much more at stake than that if I don't go.'

'OK,' Netta said, mainly to calm him down and stop him from relapsing right then and there. But also she wouldn't argue with him because she knew he would go back to court, whatever anyone said. No one would stop him. And though she feared it would kill him, just as he had predicted it would on Christmas Eve, Netta's insides swirled with admiration for him and a feeling of inadequacy for herself, which sent that urgency racing through her veins again.

The car seemed almost as full as it had been when she left for England the first time. As well as their own luggage which had been bolstered by all the Christmas gifts, Billy and Netta were given boxes of cakes by Martha and jars of pickled pork by Max. So many in fact that Netta wasn't sure if they were showering her with these delicious gifts in order to tempt her back soon or hoping she would stay away for as long as it took to consume this lot. Karl was busying himself packing all the items into the back of the little Lloyd and Netta could feel he was making a fuss in order to avoid the emotional goodbyes going on around him. However, when Billy and Netta had hugged and kissed Max and Martha yet again, there was no one left to say goodbye to but Karl, since Frieda and Erika were helping Gerhard settle back in upstairs. To Netta, the absence of her Opi and Omi was nothing short of traditional, but the void left by her mother left a bitter taste, which she guessed was intended, since they hadn't really spoken since their argument about Billy on Christmas Eve.

Karl was eventually persuaded by Martha to stop fiddling with the cases and to say goodbye. He shook Billy's hand warmly and embraced Netta, saying, 'Don't leave it too long until you come back, my dear. What happened to Gerhard made me think. I don't know how many years I've got left.'

'Oh, Opa. You've got many years left in you yet. But anyway I will... *we* will be back soon. I promise,' she smiled, swelling with the sense of security the word *we* gave her.

'Where's your bloody mother?' Max grumbled.

'Don't worry, Papa. It's OK.'

'No, it's not OK.' And he called up to the slightly open window above, 'Erika! Are you coming down?'

The response came quickly, well-rehearsed. 'My father is sick, if you haven't noticed. I need to attend to him.'

'Your daughter is leaving, if you haven't noticed. You need to attend to her too.'

'Honestly, Papa, it's—'

Netta was cut off by the sound of a horn tooting manically and a car haring down the road towards them. The second hand Hansa skidded to a halt behind the Lloyd and Anton, Anna and Sophie tumbled out, all squealing with excitement.

Netta was so happy to see them, she threw herself into their arms saying, 'Who's car is this?'

'Mine,' Anton said, his hand shooting into the air like one of the children in his class eager to answer a question.

'Since when did you have a car? Netta laughed.

'Since Christmas. Present to myself. Well, when I was sure you were going back to England I thought I'd better, otherwise we'd be stuffed for decent transport like we were last term.'

'That's all I ever was to you, wasn't it,' Netta said playfully, 'a bloody chauffeur.'

'Don't be silly,' Sophie said. 'Do you think we would have come all this way to see you off if that was so?'

'No, we're going to miss you terribly. Again,' Anton grimaced.

'Both of you,' Anna said, draping herself over Billy's shoulder.

'But be sure we are invited to the wedding. Wherever it is,' Anton said in English to Billy with a wink.

'Of course,' Billy said without hesitation or irony, which made Netta's eyes wide with a joyful panic – a panic exacerbated by the sight of Max scowling up at the room where his wife was no doubt cursing him right now; the same room where Frieda sat mortally supressed by her overbearing husband; and the sight of Martha now scolding a tutting Karl for fussing over the car again. Is this what Billy and I have got to look forward to? she thought, breathlessly.

As they all hugged and kissed noisily again, Netta said quietly to Anna, 'No Felix?'

Anna shook her head and shrugged, and Netta felt the need to look up to the window. Erika was peering out, but ducked back inside the moment she realised she'd been spotted.

'Time to go then,' she announced with a tearful smile.

Billy shook Max and Karl's hand one more time and got into the car with Netta. And they drove away. Netta glanced in the rear view mirror frequently, recalling the send-off she'd had the first time she'd left and noting how the players in this one were different. It impressed on her the inevitability of change and she wondered just who would be standing in the road the third time she left and who would be sitting in the car with her. She reached out and found Billy's hand, gripping it as one might hold onto a lifebuoy in open water.

'Is that your mate?' Billy said as they turned a corner.

Netta looked over her shoulder as they sped past a young man trying to flag them down. It was Felix. Netta pulled over and he came running back to the car. Billy wound down his window and Felix held onto the frame as he caught his breath.

'Thought I'd missed you.'

'You OK?'

'Just out of breath. Was running. Those bastards didn't pick me up.'

'They thought you didn't want to come.'

'Why wouldn't I want to come, Net? You're a friend.'

Netta smiled, wearily but warmly.

Felix had been speaking over Billy so far. But now he spoke directly to him in English. 'Billy,' he said taking a particularly deep breath, 'I like… your clothes. Very… smart.'

'Really?' Billy was flattered.

Felix nodded and offered his hand which, after a brief, cautious pause, Billy shook then leaned out of the window examining Felix's feet.

'What is it? Felix said.

'Your feet look similar to mine. The size, I mean. Would you like my boots?' he didn't wait for an answer before he started pulling off his Chelsea boots.

'Oh, no!' Felix said when he realised what Billy was doing.

'Here you go.'

'No, no, really, I could not—'

'Don't you like them?' Billy said, mock-hurt.

'I do like them. Very much. But what will you wear?'

'I've got more back there. Don't worry about me,' Billy smiled, wafting the boots under Felix's nose as if they had an irresistible smell.

After a red-faced pause during which Felix glanced at Netta to see what her take on this offering was – her mouth was hanging open in shocked amusement – Felix took the boots and thanked Billy. They shook hands again.

'Later, Felix.'

'Goodbye, Billy.'

'Bye Felix. See you soon,' Netta said.

'Take care,' he called out as Netta pulled away.

She looked in the rear view mirror as they drove off and saw Felix standing on the pavement examining the boots in a somewhat bewildered fashion.

'That was… really nice of you,' she said to Billy.

'Well, they were buggered from all that walking over the fields anyway,' Billy laughed.

18

'How was it then?' Rita said, her face beaming with anticipation.

'It was pretty amazing actually,' Billy said as he handed a box of cakes to her from the car and Netta noted with a little irritation at how surprised Billy sounded that it had been *amazing*. 'Take those inside, will you? You can have a bit if you like.'

'Ooh,' Rita said opening the box as she went inside. 'What's this?'

'Black Forest gateau, of course,' Billy said with a new found authority on all things German.

'That looks too nice to be good for you.'

'Just shut up and get it down you!'

Rita took a bite as they came into the living room. 'Oh, I miss travelling, I do. I really want to do more,' she said with a mouth full of gateau. 'I can't wait to get away again.'

Netta noticed the energy drain from Rita's voice as she said this last sentence and it made her look up from the bags she was carrying and at her friend who was holding her face as she chewed.

'Toothache?' Netta asked.

'Something like that,' Rita grimaced.

Netta thought she saw bruising around Rita's jaw, but it could have just been the terrible lack of light in the room, she told herself, since Rita was already jabbering away with her usual speed and gusto again.

'I must persuade Henry and Zelda to take me with them on the next buying trip. They reckon they're a bit strapped for cash recently so we can't all go, but I can't see why. The latest stuff is flying off the shelves apparently. I think they're just being tight, but that's the Jews for you, innit.'

'Rita!' Netta's exclamation was meant to scold her, but Rita didn't seem to notice.

'Netta, darling, how did it all go with the family and that?'

'Oh you know how families can be.'

'Tell me about it, I just had to spend Christmas with my lot. I'm not doing it again. Pain in the bloody arse the lot of them. Everyone except your Albert of course,' she said putting down the cake box and putting her hands on Billy's father's shoulders as he sat in his armchair watching the TV looking as if he hadn't moved since the last time Netta had seen him.

'Gerroff,' Albert shrugged Rita's hands away, 'You've got sticky hands now. I don't want it all over my jacket.'

'Do you want a bit of cake, Dad?' Billy asked.

'No, I don't. Bloody foreign muck. Probably poison me anyway.'

Netta sighed, 'Hello, Mr Langley.'

'How was he?' Billy asked Rita over Albert's head.

'Like I said, no trouble.'

'Course I was *no trouble*. I'm not a bleeding kid, am I?'

'Well, I don't know about that—'

'If you're not going to shut up, go in the kitchen and talk. I'm trying to watch this.'

'Ooh, charming,' Rita laughed. 'He's probably just missing Doe. Couldn't keep their hands off each other those two.'

'Piss off!' Albert spat.

Rita was delighted by this reaction and scampered into the kitchen with the cake, followed by Billy.

Netta thought that this was the perfect opportunity to give Billy's father the present she'd bought him from Dortmund. She reasoned that since he was so annoyed by Rita and Billy, she was in a position to gather numerous Brownie points by being the only person who'd done something nice for him since their arrival. 'Mr Langley, I've brought a present for you.'

Albert looked at her with a kind of disgusted surprise as she crouched next to him and handed him the box. He hesitated for a moment, then ripped it open and pulled out a snow globe in which stood a beautiful old house surrounded by pine trees all covered in a layer of snow.

'Look,' she said gently taking it from him and shaking it so the snow began to swirl around the rural scene. She watched as his eyes flashed momentarily with something. Joy? Anger? Grief? A memory?

'I don't want it,' he said pushing her hand away and boring his eyes into the TV screen.

'Netta! Netta!' Rita hissed from the kitchen, beckoning her over.

She was glad to have an excuse to leave and left the snow globe on the mantelpiece as she did so.

'Did he like his present?' Billy said absently, his mind on making cups of tea.

Rita didn't give Netta a chance to respond to him anyway. ''Ere, I was having a sherry or three with my auntie Jeanie over Christmas and she was telling me all sorts about what her husband Buster and Albert here got up to during the war.'

'Oh yes?'

'Yeah. They'd both survived Dunkirk, you see and after that they were both sent to Germany. Apparently, Jeanie said, when they rolled into Hamburg – I think it was Hamburg, but it could have been somewhere else, anyway Hamburg rings a bell, so let's say that – when they rolled into Hamburg the troops demanded that they were put up in some of the nice boarding houses that had survived the bombing and Buster and Albert ended up sharing a room in this little place run by two sisters. German of course, don't ask me their names, I can't remember now – I was already three sheets in the wind after all that sherry – but I remember this: Turns out Albert had a soft spot for one of these sisters. Buster did too, for the other one, but she wasn't interested apparently – or that may have just been Jeanie making herself feel better. I don't know, anyway – Albert only goes and falls for this other one. Buster told Jeanie he hardly saw Albert after that. He even made Buster get another room so he could have his wicked way with her every night. She lived in the same room as her sister, see, so they weren't likely to have a bit of how's your father in there, were they? Anyway the war's over eventually and the time comes for the troops to move out. And as they're packing up Albert only goes and asks the German girl to come with him, dunnee.'

'To England?' Netta said.

Rita nodded, 'Mmmm – like that was going to happen then just after the war! Anyway, she refused. They'd declared their undying love for each other and that, but she said she couldn't leave her sister, but he was welcome to come back after and be with her there.'

'So why didn't he go back. Or why didn't he just stay?'

'Well, that's what I asked Jeanie. And she said that was what she asked Buster. And he said that was what he asked Albert.'

'And what did Albert say?' Netta was hooked.

'Albert wouldn't say. It's a mystery. But Jeanie reckons he was too scared to go and live over in Germany, even if the love of his life was there.'

'Oi, she weren't the love of his life,' Billy said handing Rita a mug of tea. 'My mum was.'

'All right, his *first* love then. But anyway as she's telling me all this it all becomes clear, dunnit?'

Netta was speechless trying to envisage that grumpy old git festering in the dingy living room as a young virile lover tumbling about on starched white sheets in a sunny room in a Hamburg boarding house.

'What becomes clear?' Billy said handing another mug to Netta.

'Well, I says to Jeanie she must have been a looker, this

German girl, to make Albert fall so hard. And she says Buster showed her a photo once of the four of them – or she found it when she was going through his things and made her tell him who the girls were. And she says this German girl was about so high, mousey blonde hair, blue eyes, glasses.' Rita's eyes sparkled like a found glass slipper and she said to Netta, 'He's not nasty to you coz you're German. He's nasty to you coz you remind him of the one that got away.'

Rita grinned through the steam rising from her mug waiting for some kind of adulation for her detective work.

'Silly old sod,' was all Billy offered.

Netta didn't know why she was blushing but she blushed nevertheless and whispered, 'Poor Albert.' Then she poked her head around the kitchen door to see Albert's eyes not glued to the TV any longer, but staring longingly at the snow globe and the German boarding house locked inside.

19

The smoky air of the staffroom was rippling with nervous gossip. Netta felt it the moment she walked in. Since she had returned to the school she had still been tense whenever she walked into this room especially, but now each time she did, she channelled her inner Gerhard – that part of her that was so near the surface in Germany but seemed to sink just out of reach in England – and so she was able to walk tall and worried less about the frostiness of most of the teachers in there. Knowing Billy was not far away helped enormously too. But today, she realised very quickly, the tension in the room had nothing to do with her.

'Is everything all right?' she asked a particularly harried looking Mrs Turner.

'No it's bloody not.'

'Why?'

'Haven't you heard?'

'I just arrived.'

'Bloody inspectors are in.'

'Oh,' Netta said.

'Yes. Oh indeed! And I've got Eddie Carstairs in my class doing his best to make me look incompetent every five minutes.'

Not surprisingly, Netta could barely muster an ounce of sympathy for Mrs Turner on this issue, so she allowed herself to be distracted by other colleagues chattering around her.

'Why didn't Johnson tell us?'

'Perhaps he didn't know.'

'Of course he knew. How could he not know?'

'Why would he not tell us? He's told us in the past. If we all look like idiots today it only reflects badly on him.'

'Well, they're not coming in my class,' Mr Thorpe said. 'I don't need bloody inspecting. I should be the one doing the inspecting.'

Netta glanced at Mr Moxley, who was chewing on the fingers of one hand furiously as he scribbled marks in a pile of exercise books with the other, then she slipped out of the staffroom. She hurried to her class. Although she didn't have the same fears most of the other teachers appeared to have about the imminent unannounced inspection, she knew that her unorthodox methods were not condoned by the headmaster, who was ignorant in fact that Netta was still practising them, so she hid in the store room all the dresses and balls and tools and various other items with which the children had presented their interests and dreams to the rest of the class as they filed in.

'What are you doing, Miss?'

'I thought I was doing my bit on films today?'

'It's well cold in here Miss, can we do some more football again to warm up?'

'There's a slight change of plan today, everyone,' Netta said. 'Today there are inspectors in the school.' Netta expected the immediate murmuring and chattering which greeted her news and she gave it time to settle before she went on. 'And that's nothing to worry about for us. We will just carry on as normal. However...' She thought quickly how she could explain the hiding away of all the props and equipment to them. '... today we are going to be talking about something different. Today we are going to discuss travel. Because next term we are going to go on a trip. To Germany.'

The class erupted into a melee of hissed yeses and groaned nos.

'OK, quieten down!' Netta called out over the noise. 'Some of you are clearly happy about that. Some of you not so happy. I want to hear why.'

A few hands shot up in the air.

'But, as always, I want to hear in German.'

Some of those hands were whipped back into laps.

The trip to Germany was in fact an idea Netta had been hatching for a while, though she had yet to run it past both Mrs Turner and Mr Johnson. She expected derision from both of them, but she was quite prepared to argue, with first-hand experience, how immersion in a country, no matter how briefly, is invaluable when learning the language. However, before she had chance to talk about this much further with the class, the students were all jumping to their feet and standing to attention as the headmaster opened the door and showed a tiny mess of a man with oil-slick hair and a small moustache, which had some of the students desperately suppressing giggles, into the room. Johnson was smiling excessively, obsequiously while the inspector seemed to be trying so hard to be stern that Netta imagined her Opi's voice on Christmas Eve talking about his first interrogator in Siberia who 'thought he was a martial arts hero, but actually he was an oily flannel.'

'Miss Portner, this is Mr Spicer the inspector. Mr Spicer, Miss Portner is teaching German.'

'Oh really?' Spicer said with a twitch of his nose. 'Guten Tag, Kinder.'

All the students looked to Netta momentarily in fear, but she gave them a reassuring nod and they slowly chorused, 'Guten Tag, Herr...' Their voices tailed off bashfully, unsure of the inspector's name.

'Spicer,' Netta quickly reminded them.

And then as each child tried again from a different starting point the result was a cacophony of Spicers, Herr Spicers, Guten Tag Herr Spicers and Tags, as each child failed miserably to synchronise with the others.

Netta felt her face redden slightly, but she recovered by speaking directly to the inspector who was still looking quite cocky after his little greeting to the kids.

She said, in German, 'Ah, you speak German, Mr Spicer. That is wonderful because we only speak German in this lesson.'

Mr Spicer look horrified. He clearly had no idea what Netta had just said to him and so he nodded and twitched his nose again, which Netta was quickly learning was his approximation of a smile.

'Mr Johnson,' she continued in German, 'perhaps you could explain to Mr Spicer that since we only speak German in this lesson we will continue to do so now with your permission.'

It was Mr Johnson's turn to redden now. He laughed rather pathetically, throwing back his head and nodding as if he was in on a joke. 'Very good, Miss Portner. Well, don't mind us. You just carry on.'

'OK,' Netta clapped her hands and said in German, 'Sit down, children!'

Johnson and Spicer exchanged a knowing look since they were both proud to have guessed what, 'Setz dich, Kinder!' meant, helped rather significantly of course by the fact that an entire class of students had just sat down in response to the words.

Netta was tingling with mischief now and announced, 'Now I want one of you to come up to the front of the class and tell our guests, in German of course, exactly what you have been doing this term. Patricia, what about you?'

Patricia dutifully obeyed and proceeded to tell the inspector and headmaster all about the mannequin hiding in the store room and the way she had shown the class how to make a dress on it and how she was going to be the next Mary Quant.

'Samuel?'

Samuel got up next and related how he had taken the class outside on the playing fields and how he had shown them how many keepie-uppies he could do, counting in German obviously, and how he had even managed to explain the off side rule to them, in German too, which was a mammoth enough task in English usually.

Then Richard. Then Rebecca, each student performing wonderfully and making Netta swell with pride, while Johnson looked increasingly uncomfortable and Spicer's nose twitched epileptically.

'Trudy?' Netta said.

'Well, well,' Johnson cut in quickly before Trudy could regale them with stories of the hamster concealed in the store room. 'We really have to be going. Many more classes to see. But it has been very, erm, enlightening, I think Mr Spicer would agree.'

'Oh yes,' the tiny inspector said as he hurried out of the door which the headmaster held open for him.

Netta turned to the blackboard and said, 'The only thing he'd be good for inspecting is skirting boards.' And the entire class erupted with laughter.

20

One whiff of spring air and the pier was teeming with people. The arcades were rarely closed but now the ice cream sellers were out alongside the deck chairs set up in front of the Punch and Judy show and the photographer who'd take a picture of you and a friend with your faces sticking out of a wooden cut-out of a mermaid and King Neptune for the price of a cornet – 'Pick it up when it's developed later from the stall next to the candy floss man!'

Netta and Billy were by the darts game; that was where they'd told Terry and Rita to meet them.

'Woo-oo,' Rita sang as she waved and tottered over to them trying not to plant her heels between the gaps in the boardwalk.

'Alright, Nets?'

'Hello Rita.'

'Alright Billy?'

'Alright, Reet.'

'Bill.'

'Tel.'

'Netta.'

'Hello Terry.'

'Going to win us a teddy bear, Tel?' Rita said tugging on the sleeve of his parka like a child.

'You've got to burst three balloons with three darts to win,' Billy warned.

'So?' Terry strutted to the stall. 'That's flipping easy,' and he slammed some coins on the counter and received his darts.

'Has Billy had a go for you yet?' Rita said to Netta.

'No,' Netta said trying to sound like she didn't care – and she hadn't cared until Rita had put it in those terms. 'What do I need a big teddy bear for? I've got Billy to cuddle.' Netta laughed and was pleased to have come up with the perfect parry – perhaps a bit too perfect, she thought, since it seemed to pierce Rita's mood momentarily like Terry's first dart popping a pink balloon. As ever, Rita was quick to recover herself and she put her arms around Terry.

'He's my teddy bear, aincha, Terr—'

Terry promptly shoved her away.

'Get off, you sill moo.'

Netta saw Rita steal a glance at her as if to make sure she hadn't noticed, which of course Netta had. Rita looked queasy, as if she might be sick at any moment, but she was not to be deterred and she went back for another cuddle.

Terry shoved her harder this time.

'How can I aim straight if you're pulling me about? Do you want me to win or what?' And he raised his hand, aiming a dart at Rita who curled up and stumbled over towards the railings with a squeal as if she actually expected him to throw it at her.

'That's the way to do it,' quacked Mr Punch as he struck Judy about the face with his stick and the children in the audience laughed riotously.

Netta looked on speechless as Terry turned back to the stall and popped a blue balloon this time. As he took his final throw, Netta went over to Rita who was studying, or perhaps pretending to study, the waves below.

'Are you OK?' Netta said gently.

'Go on, Tel!' Billy shouted. 'Don't mess it up now.'

'I won't if you keep it down.'

'I'm fine,' Rita smiled unconvincingly at Netta as the third dart thudded into the wood behind an exploding red balloon.

'GET IN!' Terry boomed and Netta noticed how Rita flinched at the sound of his voice before running over to congratulate him.

'There you go, love,' the stall owner said as he handed

Rita a large blue and white teddy bear. 'I assume it's not for you,' he winked at Terry.

'No it bleeding aint,' Terry replied. 'Now, don't say I never get you nothing,' he said to Rita as the lights on the pier were turned on.

'Ah, thanks, darling,' Rita beamed and hugged the teddy.

Terry said, 'Now are we going to get a beer or what?'

Netta looked at the evening sky, how much darker and colder it seemed since the lights had come on. Yet the strings of bulbs lining every structure on the pier at first comforted her with their white glow, then reminded her of the snow lining everything in that little scene in the snow globe she'd bought for Albert. This sent her stomach somersaulting like the kids on the trampolines nearby – now she wasn't sure if she was elated or bereaved.

'You coming, Nets?' Billy called out, almost at the ballroom entrance.

'Yes,' Netta said and hurried to the door.

Terry brought the drinks over to their table on a tray. 'Two bob for a pint? Are they taking the piss?'

Billy sighed, 'Tourist price probably.'

'Well, I ain't no bleeding tourist, am I. I'm a local. I've a good mind to kick up a fuss.'

Rita urged him to sit down. 'It's not a tourist price. It's the same price in London these days. Even more in some pubs up there.'

'When do you go out to pubs in London?' Terry moaned.

Rita went pale. 'Sometimes after work with Henry and Zelda. Or when we take a new client out to lunch or something.'

'Take a client out to lunch. Oo, la di da,' Terry mocked.

'What? We do sometimes,' Rita pouted.

'Don't mind him, Reet.' Billy laughed, 'Tel's just jealous coz he's only got clients with trotters and a snout who roll about in shit all day.'

'Fuck off,' Terry said slurping at his pint in a way which Netta thought might not be out of place among his porcine *clients.*

There was a silence at the table as each of them sipped on their drinks, Rita swaying to the Doris Day ballad all the couples were dancing to and Netta examining the teddy bear, which had been given a seat of its own at the table and looked utterly lost as only teddy bears can.

'I fancy a dance,' Rita sighed as she looked up at the mirror ball in the centre of the room which bejewelled the walls with teardrops of light.

Netta noticed how her friend had been careful not to ask Terry directly to dance, no doubt dreading another rejection, and since Terry clearly had no intention of sweeping her off her feet anytime soon, Netta said, 'Me too. Come on!'

'What, me and you?' Rita laughed.

'Yes, why not? I'm sure the boys want to finish their drinks before they dance.'

'Good idea,' Billy smiled up at Netta. 'I'll need to get this down me before I've got the guts to get out there.'

'You see?' Netta said. 'So come on!'

She held out her hand to Rita and soon they were both dancing and giggling as Netta led them round the floor far from the boys. When she could barely see them anymore through the forest of dancers she felt it was safe to say, 'I'm worried about you, Rita.'

'What? Why do you say that?' Rita suddenly looked as needlessly guilty as Netta had felt the first time they'd ever met in the greengrocer's on North Street.

Netta held Rita a little closer and said very quietly, 'Life is too short.'

'For what, darling?'

'To stay with someone who hurts you.'

Rita looked up at the candy-striped canopy which was draped from the ceiling and blinked furiously. Netta realised the tide of dancers was washing them back round towards their table so she anchored herself to the spot and just swayed with Rita.

After a long pause during which Netta refused to speak, Rita said, 'I try. To leave, I mean. Every bloody weekend I swear to myself I won't do another week. I sit in the bath of a Sunday and I imagine just how I'm going to tell him. Every part of me screams to go. *Every part.* I get pains in m chest and I don't know if that's love or fear, but either way, I mean, I've got to leave him just to avoid a bloody coronary, ain't I? Do you know what, Nets, I've cried more in the months I've been with him than the rest of my life put together, I swear. But then when I'm in the bath and I'm shaving me legs and I've imagined the leaving bit – and I've managed to get away without a scratch – then I imagine my life afterwards. Without him in it. And it feels like soap in my eyes. I have to wash it out. Coz life without him, it scares me, Nets.'

'But you look scared when you're with him.'

'Can't live with him, can't live without him,' Rita laughed an empty laugh. 'All those clichés are clichés because they're true, you know.'

They danced together in silence for a few bars and Netta felt Doris Day's lyric, 'I'll never stop loving you,' pierce both their guts like a rusty arrow. Then Rita shook her head over and over again as if she was having a muted argument with herself.

'I'm not scared to be without Terry,' she said eventually, her eyes darting around the room to make sure they were not drifting back towards their table. 'I'm scared to be alone.'

Rita gripped Netta's hands so tightly it hurt, but Netta knew the worst thing she could do now was pull away, so she used the pain; she allowed it to irritate her and it kept her from crying.

'That's not the Rita I know,' Netta said.

'Ain't it?'

'The Rita I know wears a miniskirt.'

Rita looked down at her latest purchase. 'What's that got to do with the price of potatoes?'

'Pardon?'

'Oh, sorry, just one of those stupid English things again. I mean, what's me wearing this got to do with anything?'

'Well, wearing that isn't just about showing off your legs.'

'Isn't it?'

'No, it's about not hiding anymore. Not being hidden away in the kitchen or stuck feeding the baby, if you had one. It says this is not the 40s or even the 50s. It says watch out, boys, because I can take the pill if I want to! And it says you can wear what is comfortable even when this male chauvinist society tells you it's vulgar to show that much leg.'

'Well, it will be vulgar if I don't keep my figure. Let's go and have a fag.' Rita tugged Netta towards the table, but Netta stood her ground and kept her grip on her friend.

'You know all about liberation, Rita.'

'Do I?' Rita said looking over at Terry who was eyeing them over the rim of his pint.

'You taught me.'

'Don't be daft. You're the teacher, aincha.'

'You know what I mean, Rita!'

Rita stamped a heel in the dancefloor, flapped her hand and screwed up her face. Then after a cautious pause, she spoke. 'I told him once I was leaving. I did. I actually worked up the courage to do it and you know what he did?'

Netta assumed that was when she sustained the bruised jaw, but she couldn't even begin to answer Rita. She didn't want to imagine the scene.

'He cried. That's what he did. And, my God, I've never heard a grown man weep and wail like that. It near broke my bloody heart. He was begging me not to leave, actually had his hands like this.' She put her hands together in prayer. 'He bawled like a child. And then I knew I couldn't leave him. I can't leave him, Nets. Coz he's just as scared of being alone as I am. You could say we're made for each other in that way,' she smiled.

Netta tried to return the smile, but she guessed her expression would be betraying her real feelings. So she looked away and her eyes settled on Terry who was scowling in her direction and she couldn't imagine him crying like a little boy no matter how hard she tried, even though she had no doubt Rita was telling the truth. A wave of fear rushed over her as she saw Terry rise and slouch over to them. Her eyes now glued to him, she was only dimly aware that Billy had got up too and was following Terry saying something to him, though Terry didn't seem to be listening.

As he came close Netta tightened her grip on Rita's hand.

'Wanna dance?' he said squinting as the mirror ball sent those bright teardrops chasing across his face.

'Me?' said Rita.

'Well, who do you think I mean, the bloody Queen?'

'Oh,' Rita sighed. 'Oh, silly me. Yes, Terry. I'd love to dance with you.' She released her hand from Netta's and said to her, 'You see, Nets? You see. He is lovely, intee?'

Billy saved Netta from responding. 'My lady?' he said bowing slightly and holding out his hand.

Netta allowed her attention to be grabbed by this and she held Billy so closely as they began to dance, he asked, 'Everything alright, gorgeous?'

Netta nodded and smiled at Billy then she let her eyes drift over his shoulder at Rita. She was grinning up at Terry like a little girl to whom St Nikolaus had given his entire sack of gifts, and yet, Netta thought, her eyes looked just like the teddy bear's that sat at the table now all alone.

21

The presence of Mr Johnson in the staffroom made the place even more uncomfortable for Netta. He stood there apparently floating in the mist of cigarette smoke, his black gown wrapped around him, like Count Dracula after one too many pints of blood.

'If I could just have your attention for a moment,' he said, although he had everyone's attention the moment he walked in the room, except for that of Thomas Thorpe, who was wagging his finger and jabbering away at James Moxley about something he'd read in *The Sun* on his lap, which Moxley was too polite or timid to ignore with.

'Erm, Tom,' the headmaster said and, without acknowledging him, Thorpe leisurely finished his sentence and folded his arms, nodding at Johnson as if to give him permission to proceed.

'Thank you,' Johnson said with a healthy hint of sarcasm. 'Now I just *wanted* to say thanks to everyone for your efforts the other day to present the school in a positive light.'

'But do you *still* want to say it?' Netta was burning to add, pointing out the strange tendency the English have of putting statements, requests or questions in the past tense believing it somehow made the listener more receptive to them – she decided it was best not to, however.

'I know some of you were taken by surprise, as was I, and consequently the inspector did have some issues, but I have spoken to the individuals involved and we don't need to go into that here.'

Netta noticed how Moxley blushed at this and Thorpe crossed his legs and glared at Johnson, his limbs now all knotted in a perfect picture of defensiveness.

'But also,' Johnson went on, 'the inspector insisted I let

you know at this time, Mr Shaw and Mr Streeting, that your lessons were outstanding…'

Netta saw Johnson glance at her as if he was deciding whether to go on when Thorpe started gobbling to himself, and reddening much like, Netta thought, a male version of Sister Hildegarda would. 'And why do we need to go into *that* here; why couldn't those people be told individually too,' he said.

Johnson faltered slightly and Netta couldn't tell if it was because of Thorpe's outburst or because of her presence in the room, which seemed to be causing the headmaster some kind of dilemma. But he went on, 'As was… Thank you, Tom! As was… your lesson, Miss Portner. Mr Spicer described your lesson as outstanding too,' he said with some difficulty.

Netta felt as if she'd just inhaled all the second-hand smoke in the room and Thomas Thorpe barked with disdain as the rest of the staff team murmured incoherently, at least they were incoherent to Netta as her head spun with this welcome news.

'Thank you,' she mouthed and nodded at the headmaster who nodded a staccato nod back and swept out of the room. She gathered up her books and was about to go to her first class of the afternoon when Mrs Turner stopped her.

'Congratulations, Netta.'

'Thanks.'

'But commiserations to me.'

'Oh? Why?'

'I was one of those *individuals* the inspector had some *issues* with.'

'Oh, that seems… unfair,' Netta said generously without the slightest idea about her head of department's competency in the classroom.

'Well that may be so, but one thing I am very sure of is that I can't bear another minute teaching that bloody Carstairs boy.'

'Eddie?' Netta said with a genuine concern for the student.

'Yes. Is there another Carstairs in the school? God, I bloody hope not.' Turner huffed dramatically and then, lowering her voice, said in Netta's ear, 'So, I was wondering… if you wouldn't mind… taking him back.'

'Back? Into my class?'

Turner nodded with woodpecker speed. 'You'd be doing me a real favour. I wouldn't forget it in a hurry, I can tell you.' Mrs Turner even put her hand gently on Netta's forearm to try and charm her into accepting, as far as Mrs Turner had ever charmed anyone, that is.

Netta looked at the hand. Looked at the pile of books she was carrying. Looked across the room and saw Mr Thorpe looking daggers at her. Looked quickly away back at her colleague and said, 'Of course. I'd love to.'

'You'd *love* to? My God,' Turner laughed, 'I don't know what they feed you on over there in Deutschland but frankly I don't care right now. Thank you, thank you.' And she hurried out.

Netta followed, taking one more anxious look at Thorpe, whose expression was now that of someone trying to strangle her by the power of his mind alone.

22

'You'll have Turner's job in no time,' Billy said to her as they lay on Netta's bed listening to the latest Tremeloes single which Billy had just bought from a shop in The Lanes. 'And then not long after that you'll be the head.'

'Oh stop it!' Netta slapped his chest playfully.

'My wife, the headmistress!' Billy breathed at the ceiling.

Netta felt her skin shrink tightly around her bones. She didn't know how to respond. Here was Billy talking about marriage and she was yet to tell him that she loved him. She hoped he *felt* how much she loved him, but she knew sooner or later if she couldn't find the words he would doubt it and perhaps move on. She knew she had been too quiet for too long and she couldn't bear to look up at Billy's face, so she buried her head in his chest and stroked the Fred Perry logo on his polo shirt. The Tremeloes had reached the chorus and the first line seemed to Netta to be much louder than any other part of the record. They sang, 'Silence is golden…' and Netta could feel Billy's eyes on the top of her head, searching.

She floated into work every day for the next few weeks. What with the inspector's report and the weather resembling summer, she felt invincible. The only Achilles' heel for this superhero was her feelings for Billy – nothing else she craved could make her feel so weak.

'Miss Portner!' It was Billy. She liked it when he spoke to her in a professional manner in front of the students and staff. It made her feel like they shared a secret and frankly that turned her on.

'Good morning, Mr Langley,' she smirked as he intercepted her on the pathway to the main entrance.

'Can I have your assistance over here for a moment please?' he said touching her very lightly on the small of her back and directing her off the path towards those large bins that stood behind the kitchens.

'Billy!' she hissed, worrying someone might have seen his touch, but thrilled at the thought that he might be taking her behind the bins for a kiss – it wouldn't be the first time, but there were far too many students and teachers around filing into school at this time of day; they were sure to be seen. So she stopped on the path and said. 'I have to go in for registration. Perhaps I can… *assist* you later?'

Billy looked disappointed. But as Netta moved off again his expression seemed more anxious. 'No, no, this really can't wait, Miss Portner,' he said blocking her way and Netta was a little miffed; she felt he was taking the game too far now.

She frowned at him. He could barely look her in the face.

'Come this way, Nets,' he said weakly. 'It's for the best. Trust me.'

She did trust him. Implicitly. She had never trusted anyone to such an extent, even her father and mother. Especially her father and mother. But the little look he threw over his shoulder drew her attention to the foyer doors where a crowd of students was gathering, tickled by the three German military officers who stood guard there. As Netta edged past a crestfallen Billy, she could examine this strange trio more closely. They were dressed in black uniforms with red Nazi armbands, the swastika badly drawn on each in felt pen. They were giving the Nazi salute to all who entered and shouting, 'Seig Heil!' in cartoon German accents. And they were Thomas Thorpe, Eric Streeting and, with a Hitler-style moustache glued on under his nose, the deputy head Gerald Shaw. Netta couldn't believe what she was seeing. She felt sick.

'Don't go that way,' Billy implored her.

'What the… Why?' Netta said.

'It's the anniversary of D-Day, innit. So they're doing an assembly about it and…'

'Who is doing the assembly? *Them?*' Netta said, her chest heaving.

'Those oily flannels?' said a ghost of Gerhard in her ear.

'Come this way,' Billy tried one more time, but his voice was feeble with resignation now.

Netta walked quickly up the pathway towards the three Nazis.

'Seig Heil!' Mr Streeting shouted as she went through the door.

As there had been every time he had shouted it, there was a roar of laughter from the assembled kids, but this time Netta couldn't help but feel the laugh was directed at her. It rushed through her body like the January wind would as she walked along the seafront. She looked up at these teachers as she passed and caught Mr Thorpe smirking at her from beneath his Hitler hairdo. As she walked towards the headmaster's office she wished so passionately that she had listened to Billy and that she had gone with him and never seen these caricatures at the entrance. And yet, like someone who finds out their lover has been cheating, she was so glad she had discovered them now, no matter how much it hurt, because that way she could make a stand before she was made a fool of any longer. Can you imagine, she asked herself, if you had sat in that assembly in front of the whole school and witnessed that performance? The feeling of entrapment would have been overwhelming – and she was suddenly five years old again, the housekeeper her father had employed, the one her mother screamed at him about, had locked Netta in the pitch dark basement for some imagined misdemeanour. She blinked away the image of her five-year-old self and with it the tears pooling in her eyes and she rapped on the study door.

'Come!'

She entered to find Johnson straightening his tie and arranging his gown in the mirror, apparently oblivious of that eternal dusting of dandruff on his shoulders, and she had the most bizarre and inappropriate thought right then that he somehow wore the dandruff knowingly like a decorated soldier wears epaulettes.

'Ah, Miss Portner, how can I help you? And do keep it brief; we should both be in assembly in a moment.'

'Well, that is why I have come to speak to you.'

'Mmm?'

'About the assembly today.'

'Go on.'

'I believe it will be about the Normandy landings by the British in the Second World War.'

'D-Day, yes. Mr Shaw, Mr Streeting and Mr Thorpe were very keen to do it. They all served in the forces during the war, you know.'

'Have you seen how they are dressed? Have you seen what they are doing at the entrance?'

'I did have a quick look.' Johnson laughed and tore his eyes from his reflection for a moment – a thought had apparently just struck him and Netta hoped it was the obvious one. 'Oh,' he smiled at Netta. 'They don't mean any harm, you know. It's just a bit of fun.' And he turned back to mirror.

'Well, I just wanted to ask you...' *There you go*, she scolded herself, *doing that past tense thing they do. Stop being so bloody English!* 'I mean, I would like to help them with the assembly. It is quite a unique situation having me, a German, here on such an occasion. I can give a German perspective on the war during the assembly, at whichever point Mr Shaw would like me to, to provide some essential balance to the issue. It should be very educational for the students.'

'Well, I am confident neither Gerald, Eric nor Tom

would like you to make a contribution, Miss Portner, but thank you very much for offering.'

'Why wouldn't they?'

Johnson had finished his ineffectual preening, but was using the mirror to look wordlessly at Netta now.

'Why wouldn't *you*?' she added.

'The assembly is about to start, Miss Portner, we do not want to be late, do we?

Netta took a deep breath to steady her voice and said, 'I will not be attending the assembly today, Mr Johnson, unless you give me the opportunity to speak during it.'

Johnson spun round, indignant. 'Oh yes you will, young lady.'

'I'm sorry, but I cannot.'

Johnson marched to the door and held it open for her. 'Come on,' he said as if coaxing a dog.

'No, thank you, sir. I am going to go home now.'

'Go home? The day has barely begun. You will go home at four o'clock, Miss Portner, when everyone else does and not a moment before, is that clear?'

Netta wanted to scream at him, but she stopped herself. Smoothed down her skirt, adjusted her glasses and walked out of the room.

'Better,' Johnson said as he followed her. 'We will discuss this little outburst later.'

She heard the familiar buzz of the students from the hall, she saw the line of teachers waiting to file onto the stage. She watched the headmaster overtake her and strut to the front of the queue. And she carried on walking out of the front doors, down the pathway and out of the school. She heard someone call her name, but she couldn't tell if it was Johnson, Billy or someone else for her ears were ringing with injustice.

She went down to the seafront. The air there tasted of greens cooked for an English Sunday lunch, so she veered off the promenade and down to the Lyon's tea room where the air tasted of home. She instinctively looked over to the far side of the huge room as she found a table hoping that somehow Billy would be sitting there just as he had been with his sister Marnie that day in winter when Netta had come for coffee with Rita. As she imagined them sitting there, her stomach churned as it had done when she had seen the siblings together and thought Billy was cheating on her, and she cursed her parents for setting such standards in her psyche. She felt the whole world was ganging up on her today, that everyone had been out to make her miserable her whole life – even the waitress who was now asking her to sit somewhere else as the table she chose was reserved. As Netta changed seats she looked longingly across the room again. Of course there was no Billy and no Marnie, but there was Eddie Carstairs's father, sitting alone, drinking tea and sinking his teeth into a particularly sumptuous looking puff pastry oozing with custard. Netta started trembling – there was no escape from the bastards, she thought. Here was another one of them who had it in for her! Looking back on it later, she had no idea what possessed her, but with her heart racing she found herself stood by Mr Carstairs's table.

'I wanted to tell you…' she began then cursed herself for speaking in the past tense yet again. She cleared her throat. 'Do you know that Eddie is back in my class again?' She hoped this news would upset him. It was her turn to make someone's life a misery.

Carstairs looked up chewing slowly, half the pastry still in his hand. A large dollop of custard dropped onto his plate.

'Mrs Turner wanted him back with me. And he is doing very well indeed now. I thought you should know.'

'Can I get you something, madam?' said the waitress pulling out the chair opposite Carstairs, assuming she was invited to join him.

This was too good an opportunity to miss since Eddie's father looked thoroughly miffed at her intrusion, so she sat down and said, 'What's that, Mr Carstairs?' She was pointing at the cake in his hand.

'I don't know what it's called,' he growled. 'Sgot a *foreign name*.'

'It's a mille-feuille slice, madam,' the waitress said in a terrible French accent.

'I'd like one please,' Netta said. 'And a coffee.'

The waitress went to fetch her order.

'Shouldn't you be at work at this time?' Netta said, intending to remind Carstairs of what a fuss he had made about being called into the school on the morning after that dreadful parents' evening last year.

'Shouldn't you?' he countered.

She winced then stuttered, 'Day off. Sick.'

'Bloody expensive at the weekend,' said Carstairs after a pause. 'I like it in here, but at the weekend they put the prices up. It's bloody outrageous. It shouldn't apply to the likes of us, should it. We're locals, not bloody day trippers. Why should we have to pay a premium? So I pop in during the week once in a while.'

As he devoured the rest of his mille-feuille slice, Netta was knocked off balance at hearing him describe her as a local; hearing him describe her in the same breath as himself. She must have imagined it, she told herself, or perhaps his 'we' was just a figure of speech. He must have meant people like himself – white, English, Brighton natives. Whatever, this little invasion of hers was not going quite the way she planned.

He washed the pastry down with a large mouthful of tea and looked at Netta as he did so. She felt the need to say something, but she couldn't think what. The waitress came with her cake and coffee and bought her a little more time, but still nothing came to mind.

Eventually Carstairs sat back in his chair and spoke. 'I

was ten years old in 1940. It was summertime. I remember coz my mum was putting on her long white coat and trying to wrap me up too, but I whined about it being too hot, so she let me go out in just me shirt sleeves. She took me down the Hornsey Road. That's in Islington, North London, in case you didn't know. That's where we lived. Where I was born. I remember when we went out we passed by the Cole Road cattle market coz it stank. They say smell is the thing you remember most, don't they. I remember the smell of the kippers too. That's what we had gone out to buy. Kippers for tea for when me Dad got home from work. But as we're leaving the fishmongers there's this awful sound overhead. Bom-bom bom-bom. And I look up and the sky is full of white lines. White lines and planes. Everyone's talking to each other, saying that they didn't hear no siren. And the warden with his tin hat goes to Mum, "Yes, madam, there was no warning this time." And just as he says that this great big black thing comes whirring down from the heavens. And this warden shouts, "Get down!" and he bundles me and Mum behind this furniture shop. Into the workshop there. The smell of sawdust was…' He inhaled the air reliving the memory of that smell and by the look on his face Netta could tell it was delicious to that ten year old boy. '"Don't let him see you're frightened," the warden said to my Mum, you know, as if I couldn't hear him, the silly bleeder. And my mum nodded at him and I could see her trying to think of something. Anything to take my mind of the bombs. And then she unwraps the kippers and I see her hands trembling as she does it, and she says, "Look at the fishes, Pete!" And she makes them dance for me and I laugh, not coz I thought it was funny – I wasn't a baby, I was ten, for Gawd's sake! – but coz I wanted to make her feel better. I remember looking at her long white coat, all covered in muck now and I was glad I hadn't worn mine at least. Glad for her, like. Less washing. And then this bomb hit the furniture shop and everything went cloudy and quiet and stung. And I felt someone grab my hand and drag me back out into the street. When the light came back I could see it was the warden and he was telling me not to look back, so I did of course, well you do, don't you. When someone tells you not to do something, you always want to do the opposite, don't you. Well, the furniture shop was gone. And so was my mum.'

Netta reached out to pick up her cup, but she couldn't bring herself to take a sip.

'The next day there was hundreds of women marching their kids up towards the station – hundreds of women and one bloke: my dad with me, with me little gas mask rattling around in the cardboard box slung around me neck like the box on the string around the Paki's neck who used to come round the streets selling Indian toffee. So we all go up to the station to get our labels put on, and then we're sent off to Gawd knows where and I never see my old man again neither. I'd never been anywhere far without my mum or dad, except a couple of Sunday school outings. But now we're being bundled onto a train and we go past all the stations I know and then all the names seem foreign coz I've never heard of any of them. When we came to Brighton we were taken off the train, hurried across the tracks and we was put into groups, each group put into one of these squares made by iron railings. It was only the bleeding local cattle market weren't it! I recognised the smell from Cole Road. There were people milling all around. Men, women and children, but it was the women that came and did the choosing. They looked so different from any I knew in London. These women were all broad shouldered, with brown leathery faces. It took ages for me to be chosen. I hoped for a minute there that I wouldn't get chosen at all and I'd end up being sent back home to Dad. But eventually I got taken in by this woman. She was kind enough, but the local kids was always trying to beat me up coz us London kids had a reputation as toughs, you see.'

'But you stayed in Brighton?' Netta said. 'After the war. You made it your home.'

'You make the best of it, don't you. It's the British way. What choice did I have anyway? I had no one left in London to go back to. The Germans saw to that, didn't they. They destroyed my family. Destroyed my home. Killed my parents in cold blood. So excuse me, Miss Portner, if I have a problem with 'em.' He got up, scraping his chair along the floor in the way she always told her students not to. 'I better get to work.'

Netta watched as he took a few steps and stopped.

He didn't turn, but said over his shoulder, 'That Mrs Turner couldn't handle my Eddie, but she didn't want him to go back to your class, you know.'

'Really?'

'No. But I told Johnson he had to.'

Carstairs left and Netta squinted at the bright shafts of sunlight coming in through the windows.

23

The weather was good enough for Netta to stay out all day. After leaving the tea room she thought about going to the pier, but she was worried about bumping into kids from the school who might be playing truant or simply out at lunchtime. She needed to be somewhere where people were not, but she didn't want to go back to the flat yet where she so often felt hemmed in, so she drove west along the coast, past Hove, towards Shoreham. Billy had shown her a part of the beach there which was always deserted apart from the odd dog walker. It was the perfect place for them to tumble around hidden by the tall grass on the dunes, like a couple of teenagers discovering sex for the first time.

After hearing what Eddie's father had had to say she was more confused than ever. Before that, and before Christmas in Germany, and before she came to this country for the first time, she thought she was quite clear about who the toxic people were in her life, but now things were not so certain. As she sat on the dunes, looking out to sea, she wished Billy was here to roll about with – he was the one person she could always count on to make her feel better. Even when she was annoyed with Billy the person she'd turn to for comfort was Billy!

And then her heart leapt. She heard him calling her name and he was coming down the beach towards her. But his call was not the childish whine he put on when they were in each other's arms, and his walk was not the carefree stroll along the sand of their last visit here. His voice was frantic and his movements urgent, and when he reached her he stood in front of her, hands on hips, out of breath.

'Bloody hell, Netta! Where have you been?'

She looked up at his silhouette against the sun. 'Here. Mostly.'

'Well, I can see that,' he said, 'But you just... you just walked out of school. In the middle of the day.'

'It was the beginning of the day.'

'You know what I mean! What happened? I looked for you after assembly and you weren't there, I went to your classroom and Moxley was teaching your class.'

'Oh, God help them!'

'Then when I had an excuse to slip out I went to your flat, but you weren't there. I went down town, all over. I was worried sick. Why didn't you tell me you were going?'

'Oh I'm sorry,' Netta snapped up at the silhouette that didn't have Billy's face then, but her mother's five or six years ago when Netta was a teenager getting home late after a great night out with Anton, Anna and Felix – and Sophie of course, but she had left earlier in order to get home on time for her uncle. 'I had slightly more important things on my mind than informing you of my whereabouts, in case you hadn't noticed.' She scooped up a fistful of sand and threw it over her own feet – if not, it might have been at the face that was scolding her.

'But you can't just walk out.'

'Can't I? So tell me what should I have done? Huh? What should I have done? Tell me! The last time you were the victim of such insensitive racism at work what did you do? Educate me! Oh, that's right, you never have been in such a situation, so how the hell would you know what I can and can't do?'

'All right, all right, I'm sorry.' The silhouette dropped to its knees in the sand in front of her so Netta could see clearly Billy's face appealing to her now, and that should have been enough to soften her, but she wasn't ready to allow that yet. 'I know I've never had to put up with what you have here,' he said, 'but you could have got the sack, you know.'

Suddenly her mother's face was there again – not where Billy's was this time, but somewhere over his shoulder in the haze above the foamy shore. And Erika's eyebrows were raised critically, telling Netta that what Billy had just said had nothing to do with his concern for her and everything to do with his desire for her status and money.

'Oh yes,' Netta heard herself snarl, 'God forbid I get the sack, Billy. It's not like we'd go very far on your wages alone, would we.'

Billy fell back on his haunches, his mouth open, his eyes pained. Then, after one ebb and flow of the English Channel against the shingle, he snapped his mouth shut, stood up and walked to the water.

Netta watched him, wincing at the viciousness of her own words and scared that he was walking away, for good. As he threw stones into the sea, Netta heard Rita's voice in the white noise of the tide coming back to her from the other night on the pier.

'I'm not scared to be without Terry,' she had said. 'I'm scared to be alone.'

Suddenly Netta wondered if her fear then was the same as Rita's. If every couple that ever existed only ever feared loneliness and that was what kept some people together when they would be better off apart. Perhaps her mother and father were such a couple, she thought. Perhaps they would be happier apart, but they were too scared to risk it – risk leaving and finding themselves lonely. Felix came into her head then telling her she'd be better off staying in Germany than going to England. Why risk it, he'd said, when she could stay in Mengede with all the privileges afforded a teacher there?

'Stability is another word for boring to me,' she had told him, but right now after everything that had happened, she would kill for a boring bit of stability. She examined Billy's back and the way his shirt stretched over his shoulders as he threw the stones.

'What'll it be, Netta?' she said to herself. 'Stick with Billy and risk becoming like—'

A seagull screamed overhead.

'Or leave him, like you left Germany, and risk being—'

The wind filled her head with the roar of the advancing sea.

24

Billy's fears were totally legitimate, of course, and Netta shared them the next day as she went into school expecting to be turned around at the gate by an irate headmaster handing her her P45. But there was no irate headmaster at the gates. He was too busy arranging his gown in the mirror in his study, then busy leading his staff team into assembly, then humiliating the latecomers in front of the whole school, then reading from the Bible and instructing Mr Streeting to play the hymn for the day. Netta sat in her usual seat on the stage and watched as Streeting sat at the piano, just as he had done nearly every day Netta had worked here, as if the vision of him yesterday in SS uniform goose-stepping around the foyer was just a dream. She looked at Thomas Thorpe sitting in the row in front of her, his hair its usual dull thatch, not the well-greased Hitler flick of yesterday. And there was no sign of Mr Shaw's toothbrush moustache either. She waited for a summons from Mr Johnson as he passed her on his way off the stage, but it was as if he didn't even know she was there. There were the usual polite hellos and good mornings from a handful of staff and as she headed to her first lesson she wondered if yesterday had indeed been all a dream – or rather a terrible nightmare.

'Where were you yesterday, Miss?' Patricia asked as soon as Netta walked into the classroom.

'Yeah, you missed a right laugh,' said Trudy.

'Ah! So it *did* happen,' she told herself. She could always rely on the children not to shrink from the truth.

'Heil Hitler!' Peter blurted out, which raised a snort or two from the kids.

Eddie, sitting next to him, thumped his mate hard in the arm.

'Ow!' Peter yelped. 'What was that for?'

'For being a cowson,' Eddie said.

'In German please, Eddie,' Netta said as she scribbled on the blackboard.

'Du bist ein Idiot.'

'Very good. Now today we are going to talk about our friends. Eddie has already talked about his most eloquently. And I am going to continue by telling you about my friend Sophie.'

Netta left the lesson buoyed, thanks to her students' engagement with Sophie's story, but as she neared the dark windowless corridor that led to the staffroom on the left and the headmaster's study on the right, she had to fight to maintain her mood. Most of the staff would hurry through the corridor, hoping not to bump into Mr Johnson coming out of his room, otherwise they may have to make some awkward small talk with him, or worse he might delegate some undesirable duty to them. Netta was no exception but she scampered towards the staffroom on this day even quicker than usual. However, the speed with which she walked only meant that as Johnson wafted out of his study, as if cued by some malicious deity, they almost collided.

'I'm sorry,' Netta said.

'Oh, do excuse me,' Johnson said. Not, 'Slow down, Miss Portner!' or, 'So desperate for a cigarette, are we?' as Netta might have expected from him on such an occasion in the past.

And as they did that momentary dance around each other that people do as they try to decide on a direction, that momentary dance that seems to last an excruciating eternity, Netta could have sworn the headmaster's cheeks were burning red. It was difficult to tell in the gloom of the corridor, but she was sure her boss was squirming, embarrassed, unusually unsure of himself and she was also sure it had everything to do with her walking out of school yesterday. She knew now, since this would have been the perfect opportunity, that he had no intention of raising the issue with her and she assumed that was because he had come to realise she had a point. Or perhaps, she thought, it was simply that a woman had never disobeyed him in that way and he had absolutely no idea how to respond. This idea filled Netta with a mischievous bravado and she said, 'Mr Johnson?'

'Yes?'

He stopped doing the dance and she reached up and swept the dandruff from his shoulders. He watched her do it, agape.

'Some people can be so cruel,' she smiled sweetly. 'We do not want to give them an excuse to mock, do we?'

'Er... no, indeed. Erm... thank you, Miss, er...'

Netta watched with a smirk as he hurried off down the corridor into the light, glancing neurotically at his shoulders and so almost slipping over on the floor Billy had just so diligently mopped.

As she was about to turn towards the staffroom she saw Mrs Maynard the secretary coming out of her office at the top of the corridor and moving unusually fast in the direction the headmaster had fled. Netta assumed she was hurrying after Mr Johnson with a message yet, as she turned back to the staffroom, she could have sworn she heard Mrs Maynard ask a passing student if he knew where the caretaker was. Perhaps it wasn't a message for Johnson but a leak that needed urgent attention, Netta thought, and by then her feet had carried her into the fog of the staffroom where she had planned to get some marking done before her next lesson, since she had soon come to resent marking books in her own time, unpaid.

She had barely begun trying to unpick the tangle of German verbs on the first page she came to when she heard Billy's voice.

'Netta! Netta!'

He was standing in the doorway like one of the students, not daring to enter the domain of his 'betters' as Thorpe would call himself. Netta jumped up chastising him with a smile for being so familiar. 'Miss Portner, you mean, Mr Langley.'

'Whatever. Look, I haven't got time—'

Netta saw the anxiety in his eyes. 'What's wrong?'

'Can you please drive me home? I need to go right now.'

'Why?'

'It's my dad.'

'Is he OK?'

'No… I don't know.'

'Let's go,' Netta said without a second thought, ushering him out of the room.

'Don't you need to tell Mr Johnson you're going?' Billy said distractedly.

Netta glanced over her shoulder at Johnson's study door. 'No. No need.' But she looked in at the secretary as they passed. 'Mrs Maynard, I have to leave. If I am not back for fourth period would you please ask someone to cover?'

Mrs Maynard looked a little put out. 'Well, have you—'

'I have to run. Family emergency,' she said pointedly in Billy's direction and was glad to see his eyes pool with gratitude.

As they ran to the car Netta asked, 'Did Mrs Maynard let you know?'

Billy nodded.

'Who called her?'

'Marnie. She's been dropping in as often as she can to check up on him. Today when she got there he was collapsed on the floor.'

Netta swung the car out of the car park and nearly ran down the woman standing with a small suitcase at the gates. She slammed on the brakes. The woman barely moved.

'Mama!' Netta gasped as she opened the car door and stood up, one foot on the pavement one still inside the car. 'What the… What are you doing here?'

'I'd recognise that car anywhere,' Erika smiled.

If she'd seen her mother like this in her first term at St Jude's she might well have fallen into her arms crying just as she'd wanted to during all those lonely calls in the red phone box on Bedford Street, but now Netta felt a great agitation at seeing her mother here, but she had no idea whether that agitation was irritation or excitement.

'How… how did you get here?'

'On the train of course.'

'All the way?'

'Well, there was a ferry in between trains, obviously – you can't take a train through the English Channel, can you, Netta? My gosh, thank God you don't teach geography.'

'That's a long way.'

'I travelled across Germany in the winter of 1945 with you in my womb, remember? A summer jaunt across Europe these days is a walk in the park after that.'

'But why? Is Papa OK?'

'Yes, yes.'

'Opa?'

'Yes.'

'Oma?'

'Fine.'

'Opi?'

'Netta!' Erika laughed.

'Omi?'

'Netta!' Billy shouted up at her from the passenger seat. 'My dad?'

'Oh God, sorry, sorry.' Netta sat back down. Then she stood up again. 'Mama. I have to go. Billy's father has collapsed.'

'Collapsed? In what way?'

'We don't know yet, but we have to get home right now.'

'What are the symptoms?' Erika said approaching the car for the first time.

'Mama! We don't know. We have to go. Are you coming?' Netta said lifting up the seat.

Erika squeezed herself and her case into the back seat and Netta sped off.

'Oh God, drive carefully please, dear! You're on the wrong side of the road.'

'I'm not. Be quiet, please, I can't concentrate.'

'Netta, please don't tell me you're living in sin with Billy and his father!'

'Of course not. Why would you say that?'

'But you said we were going home.'

'Billy's home, not mine. Just a figure of speech.'

'Has the ambulance been called?'

'Of course it has,' Netta snapped then whispered in English to Billy, 'Did Marnie call an ambulance?'

'I bloody hope so,' Billy said, his foot pressed to the floor on an imaginary accelerator.

An ambulance was indeed parked outside the house when they arrived. Billy ran inside and Netta was hot on his heels, but she was halted by her mother shouting from the car, 'Netta. How do you get this seat up?'

Netta sighed, then huffed and puffed her way through raising the seat and assisting her mother out of the back.

'Can you get my case?'

'Mama, it can stay there.'

'But it might get stolen.'

'Who would do that?'

'I don't know. We're not in Germany now, dear.'

Netta swore under her breath, grabbed the case from the car and hurried inside. When she came into the living room she found Billy and Marnie fussing over Albert and two men in navy blue uniforms and sky blue shirts encouraging him to get onto a stretcher. He was, however, sat in his armchair as usual, telling them, in language Netta was glad her mother could not understand, to go away.

'If we get you to the hospital, sir, then the doctors can look you over and make sure everything's running smoothly. We don't want it happening again now, do we?'

'Look me over? Running smoothly? I'm not a bloody Morris Minor you know. I had a light ale and I went a bit squiffy. It's nothing I haven't done a hundred times coming out of the Bricklayer's Arms.'

'Well, perhaps you shouldn't be drinking this early in the day, sir.'

'And perhaps you should be minding your own bleeding business. Now will you please piss off and leave me in peace.'

'Dad!' Marnie blushed.

'I'm sorry about him,' Billy said to the ambulance men.

'Don't you apologise for me, it's them what should be apologising for trespassing.'

'Jesus, Dad, they're hardly trespass—'

'I don't need no hospital to tell me what's wrong with me.'

And suddenly Netta was aware of her mother striding across the room from her open suitcase, from which she had pulled her stethoscope. She placed it firmly down the front of Albert's shirt, pinning him to the armchair and he was silent for the first time since they'd arrived – stunned into silence.

'Your heart beats too fast,' she said in faltering English.

'So would yours be, if someone had just shoved their hand down your shirt,' Albert said looking up at the woman with the German accent with irritation – or was that excitement?

'Auricular fibrillations,' she said to herself, then asked Albert. 'Rheumatic fever?'

'When I was a lad, yeah,' Albert said suspiciously.

'That makes lesions on the heart. Digoxin will help,' she said to the ambulance staff. '0.25mg twice a day.'

'And who are you?' one of them said, disgruntled.

'A doctor. The G.P. can prescribe. No need for hospital.'

This made Albert's ears prick up. 'Yeah, you see? She's the doctor. No need for hospital,' he sneered at the ambulance men as Netta looked on trying to hide her smile.

25

Marnie had to get back to the kids and Netta left her mother with Billy and Albert while she went back to school to finish the day, not wanting to push her luck any further where Johnson was concerned. Albert was more than happy for Erika to stay. He had taken quite a shine to her since she had advocated for him to stay at home and not go to hospital, but also Netta suspected he was also imagining himself with the German girl from the boarding house, as if they had never parted, as if they had come to England together, just as he'd wanted, and they had grown old together here – or perhaps this was just Netta's fantasy.

'Oh, I was hoping to get a tour of your school before we went home.' Erika said as Netta got ready to go.

'Home? My flat, you mean?'

'Yes. It's a little far to go straight home to Germany today, dear.'

'Yes, yes, of course,' Netta stuttered. 'Perhaps another day for the school, OK?' she said as she left Billy's house and hurtled to the flat to tidy up and clean before she went back to school with a knot her stomach throughout that told her no matter how much she scrubbed her mother was bound to find something to criticise.

Shortly after four o'clock she picked up Erika from Billy's house and the two women drove in near silence back to George Terrace, Netta surreptitiously examining her mother's various facial expressions of distaste as they entered the building.

'Shoes off,' Netta said.

'I beg your pardon?'

'The landlord likes us to take our shoes off here before we walk up the stairs?'

'Oh does he?' Erika said without appearing to have the slightest intention of bending down to take hers off.

'*I* would like you to take off your shoes, mother,' Netta said taking off her own.

Erika tutted and sighed with teenage histrionics and then followed Netta in her stockings up to the second floor.

'Oh,' was all Erika said as she crossed the threshold. She spun round cautiously in the dingy living room, then stepped into the bedroom and, after a brief, nose-scrunched pause, she hurried to the bathroom, flattening her hands on the wall as if she expected a secret door to open and a veritable palace to be revealed beyond this mere gatehouse. 'Is this it? All of it?'

'Yes, Mama. Coffee?'

'This is where you've been living for the last year?'

'Where else? Coffee?'

Netta could feel her mother behind her now as she prepared some coffee by the sink.

'This is your kitchen?'

'You could say that.'

'When was the last time you cleaned?' Erika said pointing to the mildew between the few tiles that clung to the wall above the sink.

Netta bit down on her lip. She knew as she cleaned the tiles this morning that she should have tried harder to get the mould out, but it had been there since before she moved in. It was ingrained in the grout. To remove the mildew was to remove the grout and so the tiles would've fallen – at least, that was what she told herself whenever she thought about having to clean it.

'There wasn't even a fridge when I moved in,' she said to deflect attention from the tiles and demonstrate to her mother just how much she had improved the place. 'I had to keep the milk out there.'

'On the roof?'

Netta nodded. 'But Billy bought me this fridge. He carried it up the stairs all by himself too,' she said intending to acquire Billy some Brownie points with her mother.

However, Erika was too busy opening the fridge, examining the shelves and the congealed tomato sauce around the neck of the ketchup bottle. 'And was it as filthy as this when he bought it?'

Netta slammed the teaspoon she was using down on the tiny counter. 'Mother!' She took a deep breath in through her nose.

'Yes?'

'You never said why.'

'Why what?'

'Why you are here.'

'Why?' Erika laughed.

'Yes.'

'To see you, of course. Now, you are not, I hope, going to prepare me anything to eat in these unsanitary conditions. Let's go!'

'Where?'

'Out to dinner.'

'Well, I'm quite tired, mother. And I'm not really hungry.' Netta just wanted to crawl into her bed and hide until the morning. And then the thought struck her that she was going to have to share a bed with her mother tonight – after all, there was nowhere else for her to sleep. The thought of such intense scrutiny without respite all day and night was too much to bear.

'Well, I'm the one who's travelled halfway across Europe today and I'm not ready for bed yet. In fact, judging by the look of those blankets, it would be a good idea for us both to put it off as long as possible. And I'm starving.'

'Perhaps you'd be more comfortable in a hotel.'

'I daresay I would be, but what kind of a mother would I be leaving you to deal with this on your own?'

Netta knew she was wasting her breath so she scooped up the car keys and led her mother down the stairs again, at the bottom of which was Mr Davies, who scampered back into his flat as if he hadn't been loitering on the stairs trying to ascertain which undesirable Netta had brought home *at all hours* this time.

'Oh, evening,' he said through the crack in his door as if he'd just opened it.'

'Who's that?' Erika asked.

'The landlord,' Netta told her.

'Oh really?' she said, then stopped by Mr Davies's face and said in English. 'Shameful. Shameful!' And walked out of the house.

'What did she say?' Davies said to Netta between hacking coughs of indignity.

'I… Oh… I'm not sure… She doesn't speak English very well at all.'

'Drive up towards the train station, would you?' Erika said as Netta joined her at the car.

'Why?' Netta said excited at the thought that her mother had decided to go back to Germany tonight, even though she knew that would be impossible at this hour.

'I passed a fine looking restaurant on the way down. We could eat there.'

'Oh? What is it called?'

'I can't remember,' Erika said impatiently, but Netta had the feeling she was being evasive. 'It had a ridiculous foreign name.'

As they drove Netta wracked her brain trying to think which restaurant her mother was on about. She wanted to identify it before they got there, partly to suss out whether it was actually as fine as her mother thought it was and partly to show off her local knowledge.

'Here. Park here!'

'But that's not a restaurant, mother, that's—'

'Will you just do as you're told for once in your life, girl!'

Netta grumbled and shrugged and sighed and prepared to be smug when her mother finally realised that the shop she was leading her daughter to was not a restaurant at all, but in fact an estate agent's.

'Look!' Erika said pressing her finger up against the window.

Netta followed her gaze to a photo of a smart looking red brick semi-detached bungalow. 'What about it, mother?'

'Do you like it?'

'It looks fine, yes. But why are you showing it to me?'

Erika sighed with amused impatience at her daughter's stupidity. 'Because we want to buy it for you, of course. Your father and I.'

'What?' Netta's stomach somersaulted.

'We want to buy it for you... and Billy, of course. Eventually, I mean, if you get married. You'll need a bigger place. And frankly the quicker you move from that awful flat the better.'

Netta wasn't sure she had ever heard her mother call Billy by his name before. She wasn't sure, until then, that she even knew it. 'Are you serious?' Netta grinned.

Her mother nodded, stealing the mantle of smug from her daughter – but what a welcome and warming smugness it was. Netta pressed her hands against the window as she often had as a child outside the baker's shop in Mengede and read the text next to the photo of the bungalow.

```
Do not be misled by the trim exterior
of this modest modern res with its
dirty broken windows at the rear; all
is not well with the inside. The decor
of the nine rooms, some of which hangs
inelegantly from the walls, is revolting.
Not entirely devoid of plumbing, there
```

```
is a pathetic kitchen and one cold tap.
No bathroom, of course, but Brighton has
excellent public baths, not to mention
the English Channel. Rain sadly drips
through the ceiling onto the oilcloth.
The pock-marked basement floor indicates
a   thriving   community   of   woodworm,
otherwise there is not much wrong with
the property... Sacrifice £3,750.
```

Netta guffawed, partly disappointed, partly amused by the uncharacteristic honesty of this estate agent. Her mother just smiled at her assuming she was still reeling from the generosity of her offer. Netta read the text describing other houses in the window.

```
Erected at the end of a long reign of
increasingly warped moral and aesthetic
values, it's what you expect - hideous;
redeemed only by the integrity of the
plebs who built it - well. Originally
a one skiv Victorian lower-middle class
family res, it'll probably be snapped up
by one of the new Communications Elite,
who'll tart it up and flog it for 15
thousand. 3 normal sized bedrooms and a
fourth for an undemanding dwarf lodger,
bathroom, drawing room, breakfast room
and kitchen. Nature has fought back in
the garden - and won.
```

'Oh my God,' Netta giggled and slammed a hand over her mouth.

```
Wanted: Someone with taste, means and
a  stomach  strong  enough  to  buy  this
```

```
erstwhile  house  of  ill-repute  in  Hove.
It  is  untouched  by  the  20th  century  as
far  as  conveniences  for  even  the  basic
human  decencies  are  concerned.  Although
it  reeks  of  damp  or  worse,  the  plaster  is
coming  off  the  walls  and  daylight  peeps
through  a  hole  in  the  roof,  it  is  still
habitable  judging  by  the  bed  of  rags,  fag
ends  and  empty  bottles  in  one  corner.
Plenty  of  scope  for  the  socially  aspiring
to     express     their     decorative     taste.
Comprises  10  rather  unpleasant  rooms  with
slimy  back  yard,  £4,650  Freehold.  Tarted
up,  these  houses  make  15,000.
```

'Well, what do you think?' Erika said.

'I think it'll be a great,' Netta laughed. 'We can make it our own. Thanks, Mama!' Netta threw her arms around her mother and said over her shoulder in English, 'Thank God Billy is so good with his hands!'

'What did you say?'

'Nothing, Mama. Nothing.'

26

Netta felt her scalp tighten as she walked into Billy's house with her mother. It sounded as if Streeting, Thorpe and Shaw were in there, dressed up as Nazis again and goose stepping around the living room.

'Exterminate! Exterminate!'

'What's that?' Netta said scowling at the TV.

'*Doctor Who*,' Billy said shaking his head. 'Dad loves it.' Then he raised his voice in his father's direction, 'But it'll be turned off in a minute if he doesn't cooperate with the nurse.'

'It bleeding won't. It's my telly, not yours.'

As Netta stared bemused at the Daleks trundling across the screen she became aware of a stranger in the room wearing a white hat and apron – the nurse that Billy had mentioned.

'Come on, Mr Langley,' the district nurse said, looking rather flustered and brandishing a long hypodermic needle, 'it really will be over in a jiffy if you just—'

'You'll be over in a jiffy. Over my knee, young lady if you don't get out the bloody way.'

'What's the problem?' Erika asked Netta.

Netta in turn asked Billy and he told her that Albert had developed a chest infection which required an injection of penicillin twice a day for the next five days – in his buttocks.

The doorbell rang.

'Blimey,' Billy said, 'It's like Piccadilly Circus in here today.'

He opened the front door and Rita breezed in.

'Hello all. Oh, you must be Netta's mum. Heard so much about you, all good of course,' Rita laughed throwing a conspiratorial glance at Netta. 'I hope you're coming out with us tonight an'all. We'll show you the sights of sunny Brighton. Well, obviously it's not that sunny now but it is gone seven o'clock. She coming with us, Nets?'

'Yes, but we have a little problem to deal with here first.'

'Oh?'

Netta filled Rita in on Albert's predicament and she expected Rita to give Albert a good talking too and it would all be over in a flash, but instead Rita looked anxious.

'But Terry's waiting outside in the car. He told me to get a move on, an' all. Look, the nurse is here. She can deal with it, carncha?'

The nurse nodded unconvincingly at Rita.

Netta looked at Billy.

'Well, hang on,' he said. 'I can't just leave them like this. And I'm not even ready yet.'

When Rita looked Billy up and down and saw he was still in his work clothes she fumed, 'Oh for God's sake, Bill. You knew what time we was coming. Why couldn't you be ready?' She was shifting about the room now, between the front door and the crowd around Albert's armchair.

'I told you! Because my dad's not well and frankly that's more important right now. So if you and Terry can't wait why don't you just fuck off?'

Rita looked stunned. She looked from Billy to Netta. Netta could see from the expectation of pain behind her eyes that Rita would have been happy to wait, but it was fear that propelled her to hurry everyone along. Billy's words had clearly embarrassed and hurt her deeply, but she could only think of one response to keep herself from losing face.

'Right, I will then.'

'Go on then.'

'I will.'

'Good.'

And after a pause which said she wouldn't, she did.

Netta wanted to run after her, but Albert was raving now and she knew Billy would want her support.

'She's not a nurse,' Albert was telling Erika. 'She's a bloody spy and I ain't letting her tell me what to do and she's not sticking me with nothing.'

Erika crouched down in front of him as he spoke and she nodded gently, sympathetically. Then she told Netta to take Billy and the nurse through to the kitchen. The nurse was not too happy about this but followed Billy with a bafflement that turned into utter indignation when Erika snatched the syringe from her.

'She's a doctor,' Billy said quickly to appease the nurse who was soon placated by the offer of a chocolate digestive and a cup of tea.

From the kitchen they all peeked through the door as Erika stood in front of the TV.

'Down!' she ordered.

'What?' Albert blinked up at her.

'Trousers. Down!'

Albert's eyebrows shot up above his glasses. 'You're not sticking that in my arse!'

'Yes. Trousers down!' she said grabbing him by the wrist and pulling him up out of the armchair.

'Bloody hell!' Albert said, but there was a twinkle in his eye too which belied his protest as he stood clutching the waistband of his pyjama bottoms.

'Quick! Quick!' Erika said.

And Netta had to stop herself from shrieking as Albert's pyjama bottoms fell around his ankles and he bent over the armchair. She watched transfixed as her mother pinched some of the flesh from his right buttock between her thumb and forefinger and Albert jumped up crying, 'Bloody hell, that hurt.'

'That is not the needle.'

'You're joking.'

Erika gestured for him to bend over again, but this time

he did so with less commitment, just resting his hands on his knees. Netta remembered trying to catch a duck by the lake when she was a child – every time she got near its tail it waddled off. And now Albert was the duck; each time Erika tried to grab his flesh he waddled a little further across the room, his legs caught up in his pyjamas. But very soon he ran out of room and Erika pinned him up against the mantelpiece and sunk the needle deep into his buttock.

Albert howled and rushed back to his armchair pulling his pyjamas up as he went. 'Good boy!' she declared. 'Big baby!' Erika cooed down at him and Netta saw Albert's lips quiver like a tickled child who is trying his best to be grumpy. 'Next time, faster. OK?'

Albert nodded, rubbing his buttock.

The doorbell rang.

'Jesus, who's that now?' Billy said abandoning the teapot and going through the living room to answer the door.

'I've had my injection, son,' Albert called out proudly.

'Very good, Dad. Very good.'

It was Rita. She followed Billy inside.

'What do you want?' Billy grumbled going back to the kitchen. 'Cup of tea, Mrs Portner?'

'She'll have a coffee,' Netta said. 'I'll do it.'

'I wanted to help,' Rita said picking at the kitchen doorframe with her long red fingernail.

'I thought Terry couldn't wait,' Billy said.

'He couldn't.'

Netta suddenly began examining Rita for cuts or bruises, but she couldn't see any.

'So I told him to sling his hook.'

'Are you OK?' Netta said looking at Rita with a simmering sense of triumph.

Rita nodded, tearful with relief. Netta hugged her tightly.

'Family comes first,' Rita said over Netta's shoulder.

'And you lot are like family to me. Now make us a brew an'all will you, Billy, there's a good boy.'

Rita was bouncing around the room again in no time, chatting to the nurse who was packing up her things and putting on her coat as quickly as she could, and chatting to Erika who hadn't a clue what she was talking about, while Albert told her to be quiet so he could hear the bloody telly.

In the kitchen, as they finished their drinks, Billy said to Netta, 'I'm glad she thinks of us as family, eh?'

Netta nodded into her cup.

'You know when you told old Maynard at school you had a family emergency the other day?'

Netta nodded again.

'Well, even though I was off my head with worry about Dad, that made me so happy to hear that, you know.'

Netta nodded again. And she noticed her own hands were trembling so she gripped the mug tighter. She knew what was coming; what was forming deep inside her and curling up towards her mouth just like the steam from her mug on the outside.

'Well,' she gulped, 'you love your family, don't you, Billy. I love my family,' she said looking through to the living room where her mother perched on the arm of Albert's chair watching the end of the programme with him. 'And...' She took a deep breath to keep her voice steady. 'I love you, Billy Langley.'

'You what?' he said slamming his mug on the counter, tea slopping over the sides unnoticed.

'You heard,' she smiled. 'You heard.'

***

Lightning Source UK Ltd.
Milton Keynes UK
UKHW040738030323
417983UK00004B/298